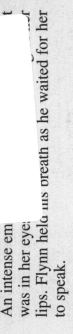

'I'm askin

An intense em
was in her eye
lips. Flynn held his breath as he waited for her
to speak.

But when she did so her voice was
contemptuous. 'Marry you?'

In that moment there was the sound of her
mother in Kaitlin's tone. The sound of that
well-bred Southern beauty in whose eyes
Flynn Henderson had never been and could
never be anything more than a simple cowboy.

'Why not?' he asked mockingly.

Rosemary Carter was born in South Africa, but has lived in Canada for many years with her husband and her three children. Although her home is on the prairies, not far from the beautiful Rockies, she still retains her love of the South African bushveld, which is why she still sometimes likes to set her stories there. Both Rosemary and her husband enjoy concerts, theatre, opera and hiking in the mountains. Reading was always her passion, and led to her first attempts at writing stories herself.

Recent titles by the same author:

COWBOY TO THE ALTAR

A HUSBAND
MADE IN TEXAS

BY
ROSEMARY CARTER

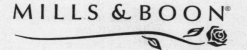

MILLS & BOON®

MILLS & BOON and MILLS & BOON with the Rose Device are registered trademarks of the publisher.

First published in Great Britain 1997
Harlequin Mills & Boon Limited,
Eton House, 18-24 Paradise Road, Richmond, Surrey TW9 1SR

© Rosemary Carter 1997

ISBN 0 263 80619 7

Set in Times Roman 10 on 10¼ pt.
02-9802-56475 C1

Printed and bound in Great Britain
by Mackays of Chatham PLC, Chatham

CHAPTER ONE

FIVE years to the day since he had left the Mullins ranch, Flynn Henderson was back. He had left the ranch on a horse, all his worldly possessions contained in two bags. He returned piloting his own plane and with a document worth a small fortune in his hip pocket.

As he brought the plane around in a great sweeping circle, he saw a flash of red and brown on the range beneath him. Round he went again, lower this time, only just clearing the tops of the trees, flying over brushlands and cattle and stretches of *mesquite*. And there it was again, clearer this time, that same red and brown. Only now he could see that the brown was the colour of a cantering horse, red the colour of its rider's blouse.

One more circle. And then he was bringing the plane to the ground, unerringly, expertly, knowing just where to land—even though he had never landed a plane there before. Through the cockpit window, still some distance from the airstrip, he saw the horse and its rider.

Would Kaitlin remember the promise he had made the last time he had seen her?

Opening the door of the plane, he leaped lithely to the ground. The horse was moving quickly. Leaning nonchalantly against the side of the plane, Flynn waited.

He could see her clearly now: the girl on the tall brown horse, blond hair streaming behind her. Memories flooded back as he watched her. He had forgotten her litheness in the saddle, the sensuous ease with which she rode, almost as if she had been born on a horse, as if she had ridden before she had walked. Which in a sense she had done, because—so legend had it—her rancher father had put her in front of him on his saddle from the moment she could sit.

5

At the edge of the airstrip, she reined in her horse. Seconds later she was running towards him. Flynn, who had thought himself hardened against all emotion, found himself sucking in his breath as she came nearer; reed-slender—had she always been quite so thin?—and graceful as a gazelle.

His mouth hardened as he remembered the promise he had made, and the reason for it. Five years ago they had humiliated him, Kaitlin Mullins and her parents, without compassion, without any thought to his feelings. Lovely Kaitlin, with whom—*stupidly*—he had imagined himself in love. On the day he left, he had vowed to come back here as owner of the ranch.

It was only more recently that he had thought of completing his revenge by laying claim to the daughter as well as the ranch. Once the idea came to him it took hold: Kaitlin Mullins would be his!

There had been bad times, rough times, days when he had been tempted to give up his plans. But always, the decision to own the ranch had given him strength and reinforced his ambitions. He had come a long way in five years, he thought wryly.

'Hello, Kaitlin,' he said.

She stopped quite still. She was tall for a woman, but at six and a half feet he towered above her, and he saw the way she tilted her head back to look at him.

Expressions came and went in her lovely almond-shaped eyes: shock, surprise, and something else, an expression that was difficult to read.

'Can it be…? Flynn…?' The words emerged slowly, almost painfully. In seconds her cheeks were drained of colour, and she seemed to sway on her feet. There was a part of Flynn that wanted very badly to reach out and steady her—but he didn't.

'Flynn.' Her voice shook. 'It is you!' She was visibly shaken.

Drily, he said, 'Yes, Kaitlin, it's me.'

She came up close to him. 'My God, I don't believe it!'

Abruptly, he stepped out of her reach. 'Why is it so hard to believe?'

Kaitlin must have registered the rebuff, for the colour returned to her cheeks. 'You're the last person I expected. And in a plane...'

'It isn't unusual for Texans to fly, Kaitlin.'

'I know that. But you're a cowboy, Flynn.'

He laughed mockingly. 'And cowboys don't fly?'

'I didn't mean—'

'What *did* you mean?' he asked deliberately.

Now that she was over her initial shock, Kaitlin was beginning to look angry, too. 'You know what I meant, Flynn, you always did.'

'You could be right. Let's try this. Cowboys are lowly, sweaty beings who know all about horses and cattle, but very little about anything else. When they go anywhere, it's usually on horseback. Pick-up truck or bus if need be. Planes and the people who fly them exist in a different world. *Your* world, Kaitlin. How am I doing so far?'

Her hands clenched at her sides as she took a step backwards. 'It's so long since we last saw each other. We should be catching up, not exchanging angry words.'

'How long exactly, Kaitlin? Do you know?'

His gaze searched the small oval-shaped face, lingering on eyes that were as green as the grass after a good spring rain, and on tendrils of fair hair shot with gold; on skin that was fresh and glowing, as if she had already spent hours riding through the brushlands, and on sweetly curved lips that seemed to have been made for a man's kisses. A potent combination.

And yet, familiar as she still was to him, he could see she had changed. The Kaitlin he remembered had had the soft slightly rounded figure of a girl soon to leave her teens: she was so thin now, and very tanned. Her body had a wiry look, that made her look athletic. Hair which used to curl around her head was drawn back in a long pony-tail, with just those few tendrils escaping onto her forehead. The clothes she wore were basic, with no concession to fashion: plaid shirt, a pair of faded jeans, and on her head a Stetson to protect her from the fierce Texas sun.

On another woman, the complete lack of artifice might have made for dowdiness. But Kaitlin had never needed

fashion or cosmetics in order to be attractive. She was still,
Flynn thought, the loveliest girl he had ever seen. She was
also enormously sexy.

'*Do* you know how long it's been?' he asked.

Her hesitation was only momentary. 'Almost five years.'

'Five years to the day, actually,' he said brusquely.

'Are you accusing me of something?'

'I remembered the date, Kaitlin.'

'I wasn't far off. Besides which, I don't happen to mark
on my calendar the anniversary of our last meeting.'

'Apparently not,' he agreed evenly.

'What brings you here, Flynn?'

'I came to see you.'

'Just like that?'

Flynn hitched his fingers beneath the belt of his leg-
hugging jeans. 'Just like that.'

'Without any notice.'

'Did I have to give you notice I was coming?'

The last remnants of her shock had gone, he saw, for
suddenly the lovely eyes were sparkling with challenge.
'After all these years? Yes, Flynn! You could have written
or at least phoned.'

'Didn't know it was necessary to do that,' he drawled.

Her head lifted haughtily. 'If you'd warned me, you'd
have been sure of a welcome.'

Flynn gave a short laugh. 'Have you become the Southern belle your mother always wanted you to be?'

'What exactly are you trying to say?'

'Expecting a man to announce his intention to visit?
Playing one suitor off against another? Demanding flattery
and lavish gifts? If so, you're looking at the wrong man,
Kaitlin Mullins. I don't have time for social niceties.'

'I'm no Southern belle,' she said abruptly. 'As for
niceties, I have no time for them either. Which is why I'll
be quite direct and ask you to leave.'

'I'm going nowhere. At least not yet.'

If she was taken aback, she did not show it. On the slender neck, the small head was erect. 'That's too bad, Flynn,
because I have things to do.'

'Busy, are you?'

'Very busy.'

'With what?'

'Nothing that would interest you,' she said defiantly.

Kaitlin was fiery and she had courage, Flynn acknowledged. Whatever ill luck adversity might have handed her, it hadn't dampened her spirit.

'Try me, Kaitlin.'

'I don't think so.' Her tone was cool. 'Sorry if I sound unwelcoming, Flynn, but I really do have things to do. Do you have access to the plane any time you want it?'

He nodded, and saw surprise in her eyes.

After a moment, she said, 'Great. Means we can plan a future visit. I'd like to talk, find out what's been happening in your life—but we'll have do it some other time.'

'You're sounding like that Southern belle again,' he mocked.

Kaitlin dropped her pretence at politeness. 'Stop putting me down!'

'When you stop putting me off.'

'I'm just suggesting we postpone the visit for another time.'

'We could, but we won't,' he said firmly. 'And you haven't told me what you're so busy with.'

'Can't you take a hint? Look, Flynn Henderson, you're wasting my time.'

'Why is it so valuable?'

Kaitlin seemed to be trying very hard to keep her temper in check. 'Phone me, Flynn, and we'll arrange something that's mutually convenient.'

She was about to jump on to the horse's back, when Flynn caught the reins in his hands.

'Mutually convenient, indeed. What kind of language is that between two people who used to be friends? More than friends, actually.'

To his satisfaction, two bright spots of red appeared in her cheeks. After a moment he went on, 'Busy with what, Kaitlin? Why won't you tell me?'

She was standing so close to him that Flynn was rocked by a host of sensations he thought he'd forgotten. He resisted the urge to pull her against him.

'Let go of the reins!' Kaitlin hissed.

Flynn was unyielding. 'Busy with what?'

Kaitlin was silent a few seconds. In the small face an expression came and went. At last, as if she understood that he would persist until she answered him, she reluctantly said, 'There's a calf...'

Her tone was so low that Flynn had to bend his head in order to hear her. The fragrance of her hair filled his nostrils.

'A calf?'

'Lost. Maybe hurt. I have to go after it. Now do you understand why I can't waste time chatting?'

Flynn decided not to ask why she had to undertake a chore normally done by one of the cowboys.

'I'll go with you,' he said.

Her hair brushed his chin as she jerked against him. 'Impossible.'

'Why?'

'It's quite a distance from here, and I'm going on horseback.'

'We'll both go on horseback, Kaitlin. And don't tell me *that's* impossible because we both know it's not.'

'We're a long way from the stables, Flynn.'

His laughter was low and mocking. 'You don't say.'

Once more he moved swiftly. Giving Kaitlin no time to react, he picked her up. The feel of her in his arms surprised him. Thin as she was, he had not expected her to be quite so fragile. Her fragility moved him, touching the edges of the bitterness that had turned him into a driven man: a bitterness that had kept him on course when he might have given up his plans.

And then he was putting her in the saddle. Seconds later he was seated behind her, his arms around her, his hands next to hers on the reins.

Kaitlin swung around in the saddle, her face so close to him that Flynn could see the lights that warmed her eyes, and the small vertical lines on those very kissable lips.

He moved, his thighs closing around hers on the saddle. Kaitlin was still looking at him as his arms tightened around her. For a moment she leaned towards him, and he held his breath, wondering if she meant to kiss him.

At the last moment she pulled back. Flynn could have kissed her, but he didn't. A low laugh erupted from his throat. Against him, Kaitlin tensed.

'Get off my horse, Flynn.' An angry order.

Once more he laughed. 'Of course—in the stables. I'll saddle another horse, and then we'll go and rescue your calf.'

'Flynn—'

'And don't try telling me I don't know my way to the stables, because I'll lay you a bet I can still get around this ranch blindfold.'

With that he dug his heels lightly into the horse's flanks. His arms were still around Kaitlin, his hands next to hers on the reins. Five years had passed since he had left the ranch, but he didn't waver once, nor did he have to ask Kaitlin for directions. He knew the way as well as if he had ridden the range yesterday.

As they left the airstrip, Flynn found himself swept with emotions he had not felt in a long time. Emotions he had not felt with any of the other women he had known over the years. Emotions he had not expected to feel with Kaitlin, not after the way she had hurt him. Her back was against his chest, her slender legs still wedged against his thighs. Her hair brushed his nose, filling his nostrils with its sweetness: he wondered whether she felt him move his lips against it. He wondered too what she was feeling, and whether she was remembering those long-ago rides through the brushlands.

Flynn knew exactly what he wanted of this woman, what he had always wanted of her. Only this time, whatever happened between Kaitlin Mullins and himself, would happen on his terms. Love would not be a factor in their relationship, for with love came vulnerability, and he would not let Kaitlin hurt him again.

When they reached the stables, Flynn loosened his arms. Lightly he leaped off the horse and reached for Kaitlin.

'I don't need help,' she told him brusquely.

'I know that,' he said, and lifted her down anyway.

For a long moment his hands remained on her waist, and his eyes held hers. Quietly he said, 'Is there something you want to tell me?'

'Should there be?' Her voice held a slight tremor.

'For one thing, maybe you'd like to explain why you're so thin?'

She slipped out of his hands, and he made no attempt to stop her. 'I've always been thin, Flynn.'

'Not like this.' And as she gave an impatient shrug, 'You forget, Kaitlin, for the last fifteen minutes I've had my arms around you. You're nothing but skin and bones.'

'How flattering.'

'Just saying it as it is. I've never forgotten the feel of you, Kaitlin.'

'Flynn—'

'The scent of your hair, and the pace of your heart.'

'Don't,' she said.

'So—why are you so thin?'

'Metabolism?' she suggested.

'Metabolism,' he repeated cynically. 'Is that what you call it? And another thing, what happened to your hands?'

'My hands?' She thrust them behind her back.

'Why are you hiding them, Kaitlin? I've had time to study them—remember?'

'Right,' she said slowly, and dropped her hands to her sides.

Flynn reached for them. The nails were very short and without any polish, and the palms were roughened by what could only be many months of hard manual labour.

'Not the hands of a Southern belle, Kaitlin.'

'No,' she agreed shortly.

'Your mother used to insist you wore gloves when you rode.'

'Yes—though I used to take them off the moment she was out of sight.'

'I remember.' This time his laughter was warm and amused. 'Hands were important to your mother.'

'Right…'

'"Katie, darling," I overheard her saying once, "a lady

must be well-groomed, and that includes her hands. Lotion, Katie, never forget your hand-lotion.'''

'Or words to that effect.'

'I don't claim that my memories are word-perfect.'

Kaitlin blinked. There was a look of such pain in her eyes that Flynn felt his heart give an unaccustomed wrench.

'My hands are no longer important to my mother. She… She died fifteen months ago.'

'So I heard.'

Her head jerked. 'You did?'

'Yes.'

'Where? From whom?'

'Someone I know.'

'And obviously you don't want to tell me. Well, never mind. Do you also know—' she swallowed hard '—that Dad died too?'

Flynn nodded.

'Not very long after Mom. Of a broken heart, I think, although it seemed like an accident at the time. I don't think he could exist without her.'

A broken heart? Maybe that was part of it, though according to sources Flynn had no reason to doubt, the bottle had contributed more than a little to the death of Kaitlin's father.

Eyes narrowing, Flynn looked down at Kaitlin: his lovely girl, his beautiful Kaitlin, always sparkling, forever laughing at some joke or another. This new vulnerability of hers touched that deep inner core which had been frozen inside him since the day he had left the ranch.

His arms lifted. He was about to pull her towards him when he remembered that whatever changes there might have been, they were probably superficial. Kaitlin Mullins was still her parents' daughter. *That* had not changed. His arms dropped to his sides.

'What is it?' she asked. 'You're so intent, Flynn. The way you're staring at me. As if you're trying to read me.'

'Read you?'

'What you see is what there is, Flynn.'

He doubted that. He gave a short laugh, hard and unamused, and Kaitlin took a quick step backwards.

'I really do have to see about that calf.' She sounded hurt.

'I said I'd go with you.'

'I don't need you, I can manage perfectly well on my own.'

'I'm going with you all the same.'

'You're a stubborn man, Flynn. But if you insist, I guess we should get a horse saddled.'

'In a moment.' He reached for her left hand. 'You're not married, Kaitlin.' He had known that, of course.

'No.'

'Why not? There must have been dozens of interested men.'

'A few.'

'Well then?'

'I refuse to marry anyone I don't love.'

'Are you telling me you've never been in love?'

Her eyes shifted. After a moment, she said, 'You ask too many questions.'

'Do I?' he drawled.

'Yes.' She paused, and looked back at him. 'How about you, Flynn? Did you never marry?'

'I did.'

An expression crossed Kaitlin's face, but it was gone before Flynn could make anything of it. 'You didn't think of bringing your wife with you today?' she asked politely.

So she didn't care that there had been another woman in his life. Foolish of him to have thought otherwise.

'Didn't have a reason to,' he said lightly. And when she looked at him questioningly, 'We're no longer together. The marriage didn't last.'

Another one of those expressions appeared in Kaitlin's eyes, though slightly different this time. 'Yes, well...' was all she said.

She jerked when he touched her chin, enfolding it in his fingers, brushing slowly once up and down her throat with his thumb.

'No questions, Kaitlin?'

She shrugged. 'Should there be?'

'Not at all interested in what I just said?'

'It's your life, Flynn, not mine.'

'True. But we were friends once. More than friends.'

'That's the second time you've reminded me.' For some reason her eyes left his once more. 'I don't know why you keep dredging up the past. Whatever there was—and it wasn't really that much—it all happened so long ago.'

Darn the woman. She could have shown at least a little interest in his marriage. He said as much.

Turning back to him, Kaitlin said brightly, 'I'm sure the story of your shattered relationship is fascinating. But right now I'm a lot more concerned about a little lost calf.'

Like her mother, Kaitlin seemed to know just how to put a man in his place.

Flynn's hand dropped. 'Which horse shall I take?' His voice was hard as he moved away from her.

Kaitlin suggested a tall stallion, and Flynn saddled it. It was some time since he had worked as a cowboy, but his passion for horses had never lessened. The horse, temperamental by nature, seemed to sense it was in the hands of a person who was more than its match, and stood still as Flynn got it ready for riding.

They were walking the horses side by side through the brushlands when Kaitlin turned in the saddle. 'When did you learn to fly, Flynn?'

'A while ago.'

'Did your new employer teach you?'

He grinned at her. 'I don't have an employer, Kaitlin.'

'You don't?'

Her eyes were so wide that Flynn laughed. 'You seem to find that more amazing than the fact that my marriage didn't last.'

'Not really,' Kaitlin said after a l[...] the look of a man who stopped ta[...] people.'

Flynn was careful not to show [...] ceptiveness. 'I found out some tim[...] work for myself.'

'What do you do, Flynn?'

'This and that.'

'Not much of an answer, and wel[...]

Flynn just grinned at Kaitlin, obviously infuriating her so much that she dug her heels into the sides of her horse, spurring it into a gallop. It didn't take Flynn long to go after her.

It was almost an hour before he saw a streak of brown in some wild grass not far from a clump of lethal-looking *mesquite*.

'There's your calf.' He gestured.

'I saw it, too.'

'It's quite safe right now, busy grazing and with its mind on its food. Still, it's lucky to be on its feet. Fifty yards more to the left, all those spiky branches—and your calf could have had its neck slashed.'

'As if I don't know that,' Kaitlin responded grimly. 'Why do you think I was so desperate to find it?'

Kaitlin was uncoiling her lariat when Flynn leaned towards her and tugged it from her hands.

'What do you think you're doing now?' Green eyes were outraged.

Flynn laughed. 'Isn't it obvious? I'm going to rope a calf.'

'I didn't ask you to. Give me back the rope, Flynn.'

'I'm afraid not.'

'*Flynn*!' It was Kaitlin's turn to lean towards him, but he held the lariat just out of her reach.

'Think I don't know how to rope an animal, Flynn?'

'I'll take your word for it, but I didn't come along just for the ride.'

'I keep telling you, I don't need your help!' She threw the words at him.

For a long moment Flynn studied the lithe figure, determination and defiance in every feminine line and angle. God, but she was an aggravating female, she'd be nothing but trouble to any man foolish enough to try and make a ⟨ ⟩e with her. But, darn it, she was sexy!

⟨ ⟩e had registered the searching gaze. 'What?'

⟨ ⟩er figured you for a cowgirl, Kaitlin.'

⟨ ⟩ you should have.'

⟨ ⟩cow*boys*—why isn't one of them out

'I...' Kaitlin hesitated. 'I wanted to do it myself.'

Flynn gave the lariat an expert twirl. 'Come to think of it, I haven't seen a single cowboy since I got here.'

Kaitlin looked away from him. 'We're a little short-handed at the moment.'

'That's all it is?'

'What else should there be?' But there was a slight quiver in her tone.

'That's what I want you to tell me, Kaitlin.'

Her chin lifted. 'There are cowboys at the ranch. Had I known how eager you were to meet them, I'd have organized a welcome committee. As it is—' she shrugged '—there's nothing to tell.'

'I see.'

'The calf, Flynn. If you're not going to rope it, I will.'

His eyes went to arms that were so slender, they looked as if they might snap if a man held them too tightly.

'You're as fragile as a bird, Kaitlin. You don't look as if you could wield anything bigger than an eyebrow pencil, much less a lariat.'

'I guess looks are deceptive, because I don't own an eyebrow pencil and I'm really quite strong. Are you going to give me the lariat, Flynn?'

'Sure,' he grinned, 'when I've roped the calf.'

'You're a pilot now, not a cowboy,' she taunted.

His grin deepened. 'Once a cowboy, always a cowboy.'

'How long since you did any roping?'

'It doesn't matter how long—there are things you never forget.' In a new tone he added, 'Just as there are things that you think about long after they've vanished from your life.'

His eyes were on her face, lingering deliberately on lips that were sweeter than any he had tasted in the la_t_ years. The Kaitlin he had known five years earlier, jus_ _ _n at the time, had been eager, wild and passionate_ _ something tighten inside him at the memory.

Beneath his gaze, Kaitlin's expression char_ _ turned suddenly stormy, while at the base o_ pulse-beat quickened. On the reins, her ha_ knuckled. She had the look of a woman w_ with some private emotion of her own, though what that was Flynn could not guess.

'I don't want my calf harmed,' she said at last.

'It won't be.'

'I mean it, Flynn.'

'If I harm it, I promise to get you another.'

'Don't think I wouldn't hold you to it,' she shouted as he rode after the calf, swinging the lariat as he went.

The small animal didn't have time to be scared as Flynn looped the lariat deftly over its head. Seconds later, he was reining in his horse beside Kaitlin's, holding the squirming calf firmly on the saddle.

His eyes sparkled. 'Confused, but not hurt.'

'Thanks.'

'No thanks necessary—I enjoyed myself.'

'So I saw.'

'It's as I said, Kaitlin—once a cowboy, always a cowboy.'

Her gaze was thoughtful. 'I believe you've been more than that, Flynn.'

His eyes were on hers. 'Meaning?' he asked, in a tone that gave nothing away.

'That was quite a performance. Over the years, I've seen hundreds of cowboys at work, and you beat them all for dexterity and speed.'

'You don't say,' he said lightly.

'I believe you've been on the rodeo circuit, Flynn.' And when he didn't answer, 'You have, haven't you?'

'You could be right.'

'A rodeo rider. Well!'

He danced her a laughing look. 'I think this baby will be happy to get back to its mamma, Kaitlin.'

'And I recognize a change of subject when I hear it,' she said saucily.

They rode back, in a slightly different direction this time, for they had to deposit the calf with its herd.

Flynn grew sombre as he took in his surroundings. At ˑˑde, Kaitlin said, 'You're looking at the mesquite.'

ˑˑ's much more of it than I remember.'

Kaitlin shrugged, but her tone was unhappy. 'You know how it is with the spiky stuff: it's a devil to get rid of.'

'Scourge of the Texas rancher,' Flynn agreed. 'But it was never as bad as this, Kaitlin. Your father used to make an effort to keep it under control, at least he did when I worked here.'

Once more Kaitlin's hands tightened on the reins. 'I'm doing my best.'

'Are you?'

She looked away from him, but not before Flynn caught the glimmer of tears in the lovely green eyes. The breath caught in his throat. Flynn had good reason to be hostile towards Kaitlin Mullins. He sure as hell did not want to be affected in any way by her distress. And yet, despite everything, her distress moved him more than he cared to admit to himself.

'*Are* you trying, Kaitlin?' he asked quietly.

She swung around, anger chasing the pain from her eyes. 'Yes, damn you, Flynn, I am!'

'It isn't good enough.'

'Maybe it isn't. Fact is, this is *my* range now, *my* ranch. And even if I'm overrun by *mesquite*, it's none of your business!'

Once more he studied her: the too thin figure; eyes which, though they were as beautiful as ever, were shadowed with fatigue; clothes which had seen better days.

Kaitlin gave her head a determined shake. 'It isn't your business,' she repeated.

Flynn turned his horse away from hers. 'I think it's time we took the calf back where it belongs.'

'My thought exactly.'

Another twenty minutes of fast riding brought them to the herd where mother and baby were reunited.

Back at the stables, Flynn jumped off his horse. He reached for Kaitlin, but with a quick little twist of the body she slipped out of his hands and leaped off her horse.

Flynn grinned at her. 'Cowgirl.'

'That's what I am,' she said tartly.

'A very pretty cowgirl.'

'You've learned how to flatter a woman, Flynn.' Kaitl

made a show of looking at her watch. 'It's getting late. I'll go get the Jeep and run you over to the airstrip.'

'What's your hurry?'

'You won't want to fly in the dark.'

'Wouldn't bother me in the least if I did. Let's go to the house, Kaitlin.'

'Flynn…'

'You know very well that I'm here to talk.'

He thought he saw an involuntary little shiver run through her before she said, 'Another time.'

'Today,' he answered her firmly.

Still she tried. 'It really isn't convenient.'

'You have your calf safely back. What excuse do you have now? I'm sure you must have thought of one.'

Her head jerked. 'What are you saying, Flynn?'

'Don't tell me you've forgotten the girl who thought the eager cowboy would come running every time she beckoned. That he would disappear from the scene when it didn't suit her to have him around.'

Kaitlin's face whitened. 'It was never like that.'

'Wasn't it, Kaitlin? Your memory is letting you down if you think otherwise.'

'My memory is just fine, thank you very much. But you have one huge chip on your shoulder. I think you should leave now, Flynn.'

'I'll leave when we've talked. And don't tell me again to phone you: you'll always find some reason to put me off.'

She hesitated. 'Flynn—'

'We'll talk today, Kaitlin. I have no intention of leaving till we do.'

CHAPTER TWO

'MAKE yourself comfortable, Flynn. There's beer in the fridge.'

'You're not going to join me?'

'I've spent the morning in the sun. I need to shower and change into other clothes.'

'Can I help?'

Flynn was grinning, an inexplicably wicked look in the dark eyes. Great dark eyes, just as Kaitlin remembered them, with golden glints where the light caught them, and long thick lashes that had always seemed wasted on a man. His shoulder-length hair was as dark as his eyes, thick and glossy, tempting a woman to bury her fingers in it.

Looking up at Flynn, Kaitlin tried to remember if he had always been quite so tall. His shoulders had been broad, but surely they had become even broader, emphasizing the length of his legs and the narrowness of his hips. And the look of strength and toughness, of utter self-confidence, that was new too: as was an aura of danger that was spine-tinglingly sexy.

Already she was reacting to him. Just a short time in his company, and a core of femininity that had been dormant deep inside her was awakening. *Be careful*, Kaitlin sent herself the mental warning.

Why was he here? That was the question she had been asking herself over and over again from the moment she had laid eyes on him two hours earlier. The question that spoiled her pleasure at seeing him again.

Five years ago he had walked out of her life, Flynn Henderson, with whom she had been so deeply in love that she could not have imagined herself sharing her life with anyone else.

Even now, so many years later, she still had nightmares

about that dreadful evening. There were times when she
jerked upright in bed, damp with sweat, heart pounding,
knowing that once again she had dreamed about Flynn.
Even in the daytime, she had only to close her eyes to
picture him at the Formica table of the bar, his expression
arrogant and mocking: on his lap a red-haired woman, her
face plastered with too much make-up, her head cradled
lovingly against his chest. Flynn should have been at
Kaitlin's party—why had he been with that dreadful
woman instead?

Kaitlin had managed to keep her head high as she fled
from the bar. But she had wept all the way back to the
ranch.

In the years since then, nobody had ever hurt her as much
again as Flynn had hurt her that night. One thing was certain, she decided grimly, she must not let it happen again.

Her expression was hard as she looked at him. Five years
without an explanation or a word of apology. And now here
he was, on her ranch, expecting her to welcome him. *The
utter nerve of the man*!

'Thanks,' she said, 'but I'll get myself something to
drink when I'm ready for it. I'm not much of a beer-drinker
anyway.'

'I wasn't thinking of beer. Thought you might like me
to wash your back for you.'

In a second, a flood of heat cascaded through Kaitlin's
body. Keeping her eyes averted from Flynn's, she said,
'You don't really expect an answer.'

'Don't I?' His tone was so seductive that Kaitlin had to
suppress an involuntary shiver.

'I'm sure you don't,' she said shortly.

'Wouldn't be the first time I've washed your back,
Kaitlin.'

Glad that her face was turned from his, she closed her
eyes for a brief moment. It horrified her to realize that despite her resolve not to let him get to her, his sexual attraction was as powerful as ever. More powerful even.

'Don't tell me you've forgotten, Kaitlin.'

'That was different,' she muttered unsteadily.

'Then you do remember.'

Kaitlin swallowed hard. 'You know what happened, Flynn. I'd fallen, my back was all scratched up. It... It was important to get the grit out of the scratches. It could have gotten infected...'

'Your parents were out and you sneaked me into the house.'

'Yes...'

'You got into the bath.'

'The way you make it sound! I had my clothes on, Flynn.' Tersely she added, 'To begin with, anyway. And when I did get undressed, it was only because my blouse was getting so wet.'

Flynn laughed, a low husky sound that made her shiver. 'I'll never forget the moment when you stripped.' His voice deepened. 'I can still feel your soapy skin beneath my fingers.'

As she could still feel his fingers sliding over her wet skin: sexy, and so exciting that her body had burned with desire for him.

Involuntarily, Kaitlin's eyes went to Flynn's hands. When she lifted her head a moment later, she found him watching her, his expression enigmatic. *Did he know what she was thinking?*

'That's enough!' Kaitlin ground out hoarsely.

But Flynn ignored the protest. Closing the distance between them, he cupped her face in his hands. 'I was washing your back, and it didn't take long before I was wet, too. And then I was in the bath with you, and—'

'There wasn't much water in the bath,' she reminded him hoarsely. 'And whatever you may be trying to insinuate now, you were only trying to help me.'

The pressure of the fingers on her face increased, sending shock waves of excitement cascading through her. Flynn said, 'It might have been that way at the start. But you wanted more than my help, even if you were playing for time. We both did.'

Restlessly Kaitlin shifted her feet, only to regret the movement when she found that it brought her closer to Flynn. Though he was only holding her face, she was aware of every inch of the long body, from the rock-hard chest to the corded muscles of his legs. She felt his breath stir her hair.

A sudden fire burned deep in her loins. She couldn't remember the last time she had been so aware of the demands of her own body. Aware of a man… For the last year she had barely thought of men: there were so many other, more serious matters on her mind.

'If I'd had my way, Kaitlin, we'd have filled the bath to the top and lain together in the water. And then we'd have made love.'

'Don't you know that you can't rewrite history?' It took all her strength to keep her voice from shaking.

'Maybe not, but it's always possible to create new history.'

Flynn's voice was almost unbearably seductive. Inside Kaitlin the fire was turning into a conflagration. But she didn't want to be aroused. Not when the man was Flynn.

'New history? Oh no, I don't think so,' she said, as firmly as she could.

'Do you remember how we used to kiss, Kaitlin? Don't shake your head at me, because I know you remember.'

For some reason she seemed unable to move away from him: it was as if her brain refused to send the right messages to her legs. 'Flynn—'

'But kissing was never enough. We both wanted so much more.'

She couldn't deny it, because they had talked about it so often. God, how she had wanted to make love with him! Two young people, madly attracted to each other. Kaitlin, just turned eighteen, Flynn going on twenty-four. Hormones crying out to each other. Standing so close to him, listening to the things he said, the desire she had experienced then gripped her again now. The intensity of her feelings shocked her.

'It all happened so long ago,' she said over a dry throat. 'I don't see any point in rehashing it.'

But Flynn persisted. 'You said we had to wait another week, I thought we'd already waited as long as we had to.'

She had wanted be quite certain of his commitment before letting him make love to her. A lifetime commitment.

What better time to announce their engagement than on the night of her party? They hadn't exactly decided on an engagement—at least not in so many words—but they had spoken so often of marriage. Kaitlin had been as sure of Flynn's feelings for her as she was of hers for him.

'I remember...' she said.

'And then your parents drove up when we weren't expecting them.'

He came closer still. His lips were temptingly near hers: another half inch and their mouths would be touching. It would be so easy to kiss him. Just in time, she remembered what had happened on her horse an hour earlier, and how humiliated she had been by Flynn's reaction. She was in no mood for another rejection.

She threw back her head. 'You made a quick exit that afternoon,' she taunted.

'Your father would have gone for his gun if I hadn't.'

Her father had been possessed of a hot temper. 'He'd have done just that,' she agreed.

Flynn's hand dropped from her chin, leaving a warm spot where it had been. He took a step backwards.

'The hired help having the gall to make love to the boss's daughter.' His lips tightened, and for a moment there was an expression of intense anger in his eyes. 'What you should know, Kaitlin, is that I'm not the naive young cowboy I was then. It's been a long time since I've been intimidated by anyone. I don't run any longer.'

The sureness in his tone caught her: it was as unfamiliar to her as the suggestion of arrogance and the striking look of success. This older, tougher, devastatingly attractive Flynn was not the handsome young cowboy who had left the ranch five years earlier, taking her heart with him.

Flynn had always been attractive, but now his sexuality was as much a part of him as a second skin: coupled with that aura of danger which never seemed to leave him, it made for a potent combination.

Kaitlin lifted her chin in a challenge of her own. 'You never run, Flynn? Not even when a man comes after you with a gun?'

'Not even then.'

'Sounds as if you've had your share of adventure. You must have quite a love-life.' A deliberately bright smile hid Kaitlin's pain.

He grinned. 'Put it this way, I've learned to handle myself. Men like your father don't frighten me.'

Looking at the rugged face of her first love—her *only* love, if she was honest with herself—it was easy to believe that there wasn't a person alive who could frighten him.

'I won't run away next time I want you, Kaitlin.'

Kaitlin—and how many other women? For Flynn had not denied having an active love-life. 'There won't be a next time,' she warned.

'There could be.'

She increased the distance between them. 'No.'

'Why not?'

'No reason why there should be. We live in different worlds, Flynn.'

'That again—Kaitlin Mullins and the hired man,' he mocked.

She threw him a fierce look. 'You're not a hired man, you've made that quite clear. And whatever you choose to believe about me, Flynn, I'm not a snob. I never was. I'd have thought that was one thing you remembered about me. If I wanted you, your status wouldn't matter.'

'Isn't that a relief,' he said drily. 'In the circumstances, you might even think again about letting me wash your back. Who knows what it could lead to?'

God, but she was tempted! She took a step towards him—then stepped quickly backwards. 'What does it take to get through to you, Flynn Henderson?' Furiously, she threw the words at him. 'You don't seem to have heard a word I said!'

'Think what fun we'd have, Kaitlin.'

'I don't have to think about it,' she informed him loftily, glad that her hands were in the pockets of her jeans, where he could not see their trembling.

'Why not?'

She gave it to him straight. 'I'm choosy about the men I associate with.'

But Flynn was not so easily deterred. Once more he

reached for her, his fingers going to her throat this time, moving up and down in slow brushstrokes. Kaitlin thought the sensuousness of it would drive her out of her mind.

'You chose me once, Kaitlin.'

'I know that, Flynn.' It was getting more and more difficult to speak normally. 'But whatever there might have been between us once, it's all in the past now. We're no longer even the same people we were then. One brief meeting doesn't change the fact that we've become strangers.'

There was a glimmer in the dark eyes looking down at Kaitlin: eyes that seemed to penetrate the superficialities of hair and skin to the very core of her being. At the same time, the sensuous finger was still continuing its nerve-inflaming path.

'Have your shower then. Alone if you must,' he said at last. 'When you've finished, we'll talk.'

Flynn was at the window, beer-mug in hand, when Kaitlin came back into the room. For a long moment she stood quite still, her gaze riveted on the tall, loose-limbed figure, tough as a mountain lion, sleek as a panther.

There was something disturbingly ominous about Flynn's unexpected arrival at the ranch. Kaitlin straightened her shoulders as she reminded herself to be on her guard with him. At the same time, she knew already that this wasn't going to be easy.

'Flynn...' she said.

He turned, lips pursed, as if to whistle. But the whistle died as he came towards her.

Not for the first time that day Kaitlin saw his eyes go over her. She made herself stand very still as he studied her. Fair hair, almost gold, had been released from its ponytail: slightly damp still from the shower, it framed an oval-shaped face and hung in shining waves to Kaitlin's shoulders. Green eyes shimmered beneath a dusting of eyeshadow, and her lips had been touched with a coral gloss. Kaitlin had discarded her jeans in favour of a white sun-dress with narrow shoulder straps and a skirt that swirled from a tiny belted waist, and on her feet were a pair of open-toed sandals.

The silent examination seemed to go on forever, but apart from a slight flicker of the eyes, Flynn's expression remained impersonal. She had been a *fool* to go to so much trouble, Kaitlin thought grimly. *How could she have been so foolish when she sensed he was dangerous*? Had her brain temporarily stopped its proper functioning?

Briskly, she said, 'I'm glad to see you got yourself a beer. I'm thirsty, too, so I'll just—'

Flynn interrupted the flow of words. 'What happened to the cowgirl?' he asked softly.

The look in his eyes was all at once far from impersonal. Kaitlin found she could not hold it for more than a few seconds.

'A cowgirl is still a woman.' She hoped he did not notice that her voice shook.

Taking a strand of blond hair, he wound it around one of his fingers. 'A very beautiful woman,' he murmured.

Something unnerving, purely sexual in nature, crackled in the air between them. Kaitlin had a sense that things were moving a little too quickly. More than ever, she wished she had changed into more unfeminine attire.

She stepped away from Flynn, feeling the slight tug on her hair as it pulled away from his fingers. 'You haven't told me why you're here,' she said.

It seemed to her that a new expression came into his eyes. 'I guess I haven't,' he drawled.

That expression, as much as his tone, made the hair prickle on Kaitlin's neck. She could not have explained her uneasiness, the feeling that she was not, after all, ready to hear what he had to say. She decided to play for time. 'It'll be dark soon.'

'So you've said already.' His tone was sardonic. 'Are you really so concerned with my safety?'

His arrogance was infuriating. 'Lord, no, Flynn, why on earth would I be concerned about you? You seem perfectly well able to take care of yourself. I'm not equipped for overnight guests, that's all.'

'Why don't you sit down, Kaitlin?'

Kaitlin did not like the sound of the words or the tone: they sounded a little too serious, somehow threatening. Still playing for time, she poured herself a glass of cool fruit juice before sitting down on a chair by the window. Flynn seated himself near her, long legs stretched out in front of him.

Steady eyes met Kaitlin's. 'Any idea why I'm here?' he asked.

She shook her head. 'Should I have?'

'I'm wondering whether Bill Seally has been in touch with you.'

'*Bill*?' At sound of the name, Kaitlin jerked in her seat.

That morning, as on so many other mornings, she had woken and thought about Bill. Bill Seally. The ranch. The mortgage. Bill, friend of the family for as long as Kaitlin could remember, and holder of the ranch mortgage, had not pressed her hard for payment.

Kaitlin had often been grateful for the fact that Bill had been able to finance her father personally when money was short, that Dad had not had to go to a bank for a loan. Bill seemed to understand the gravity of her situation, he knew how hard it had been for her to take over the running of the ranch. Scrupulous about her obligations, Kaitlin made a point of paying Bill whenever there was money left over after the running expenses of the ranch had been met. Still, there had been times, especially lately, when it had been impossible for her to come up with the money.

'What on earth does Bill have to do with your visit?' she asked tensely.

'We've done some business together.'

The eyes that held hers were cool as steel. The uneasy sensation was even stronger now. 'What sort of business, Flynn?'

'Can you guess, Kaitlin?'

An idea came to mind, but it was so horrific that Kaitlin could not bear to give it credence. She made an effort to suppress a great inner trembling.

'I'm not in the mood for guessing games,' she said flatly.

'Fine.' Flynn's tone was crisp. 'In that case, I won't keep

you in suspense. I'm here to talk about Bill Seally and the mortgage over your ranch.'

Kaitlin's eyes were troubled. 'What about Bill?'

'When was the last time you made a payment, Kaitlin?'

'I don't think that concerns you.'

'Believe me, it does. When was it, Kaitlin?'

'Two months ago.' She hesitated. 'Maybe three…'

'A long time to be overdue in your obligations.'

Kaitlin pushed a hand through her hair. 'Do you think I don't know that? I try to pay Bill whenever I can. Fact is…' She paused.

'Go on.'

'There've been problems,' she said after a moment.

One dark eyebrow lifted. 'What kind of problems?'

'Since Dad died—' Abruptly, Kaitlin stopped the flow of the sentence.

She didn't owe it to Flynn to tell him how badly her father had mismanaged his affairs, so that after his death Kaitlin had become heir to a host of financial difficulties. In fact, why should Flynn know anything about a situation that was growing more serious every day?

'Problems that should be of no interest to you,' she said flatly.

But Flynn was undeterred. 'I wouldn't ask if I wasn't interested.'

Dodging the issue was getting her nowhere, Kaitlin realized. Flynn would simply continue to badger her until she gave him an answer: for some reason, he seemed to feel he was entitled to one.

Even then she took her time about speaking. Looking around the room, she took in the small details of her surroundings which she was normally too busy to notice: a picture that hung crookedly on the wall, a cobweb in one corner of the ceiling, a vase in which the flowers were dying. Signs of neglect that would have been unthinkable when her mother was alive. If only these small lapses of efficiency were all Kaitlin had to deal with.

'Bill isn't too concerned about my problems, so why should you be?' she asked at last. 'Bill Seally has always been understanding. He's never minded if a payment was late.'

'Don't be too sure of that.'

'What are you trying to say?'

'Even the most understanding of men get nervous about money.'

'Bill told you that?' Kaitlin demanded.

'In slightly different words.'

'He sent you here?' Her lips were suddenly stiff. 'Bill told you to come to the ranch and remind me about paying? It's so unlike him.' She stood up abruptly. 'He needn't have done that, Flynn. He could have called me, could have spoken to me. We've never needed to communicate through a third party. We'll work things out.'

'Sit down, Kaitlin,' Flynn said, not unkindly.

'No! I need to speak to Bill.'

She was moving towards the phone when a hand snaked around her wrist, the cool fingers like ice against her burning skin. 'Wait, Kaitlin. There's more.'

'Don't you understand? Whatever it is, I want to hear it from Bill, not from you. I've never liked messages.' Something drove her to add, 'Or, in this case, the messenger.'

Flynn did not rise to the insult. 'Sit, Kaitlin.'

His tone held a sure authority that made her feel cold. Slowly, unwillingly, only because she realized that in the end she would have to hear him out, she eventually did as he asked. 'Well?'

Flynn let her have it straight. 'I own the mortgage now, Kaitlin.'

Silence greeted the words. A shocked silence. A silence that lasted almost a minute. The blood drained from Kaitlin's face, leaving her face ashen. Her body was so rigid that she could not have moved if her life had depended on it.

'You had no idea?' Flynn asked at last.

'None,' she whispered.

Once more there was silence.

This time Kaitlin spoke first. 'Why didn't Bill tell me?'

'For one thing, I asked him not to.'

'*Why*? Why would you be so cruel?'

'Cruel?' The dark eyes glittered.

'You must have known I'd be shocked.'

'Would you have been less shocked if Bill had given you the news himself?'

'I don't know… Maybe… At least I'd have had time to think about it before…' She stopped.

'Before?' he prompted.

'Before seeing you.'

'Do you really think it would have made a difference?'

Kaitlin's face lifted to meet Flynn's gaze. For one awful moment she wondered if she was going to cry: tears were gathering at the back of her eyes and a sob rose in her throat. But she managed to stop herself from weeping as anger stirred.

Furiously, she said, 'You could have given me some warning before flying in here like some feudal lord. Any decent person would have let me know in advance. And don't give me any of that nonsense about Southern belles— you knew how shocked I'd be when I heard what you had to say. The least, the very least you could have done, Flynn, was to tell me why you were coming.' Her eyes sparkled with outrage and defiance. 'This is still my ranch, Flynn. Whatever piece of paper you may own, this ranch is mine, and you are not welcome here.'

His gaze flicked her face. 'What's your point, Kaitlin?'

'Arriving here out of the blue. Ordering Bill not talk to me. Knowing how shocked I'd be when I found out what you'd been up to. My God, Flynn, you must have been laughing your head off at me!'

'Is that what you think, Kaitlin?'

'I think you could have found a less dramatic way of telling me my fate.'

'Now who's being dramatic? It's not as if the idea of a mortgage is new to you. Only the identity of the person holding it has changed.'

On the face of it, what he was saying was perfectly true. The ranch was heavily mortgaged, a fact that was never very far from her mind. Why then did she have this dread feeling that her world would never be the same again?

All at once, Kaitlin felt as if she could take no more.

She had managed, somehow, to endure the loss of her parents and the hardships of the ranch. And now here was Flynn. Tough, arrogant, unyielding Flynn. He would not be as understanding as Bill had always been: if anything, he would be ruthless. Unable to hold his cool-eyed gaze a second longer, she dropped her head and put her face in her hands.

She flinched when his arm went around her shoulders. She hadn't realized that he had left his chair.

'Kaitlin,' he said softly. 'Are you crying?'

She lifted her head to look at him. Her eyes were dazed and a little damp, but she was able to say, 'I don't cry that easily.'

'You never did, that's one of the things I remember about you. You always were a gutsy girl.'

Gutsy… At this moment, when she did not know how to defend the attack on her beloved home, Kaitlin felt anything but gutsy. She yearned to lean against the hard body, to bury herself in it, to seek warming comfort from the man who had meant so much to her once. Yearnings that were quite inappropriate, for as she looked into the rugged face she knew that Flynn had become her adversary.

She twisted away from him. 'Bill should have told me.' Her voice was low. 'Why didn't he tell me, Flynn?'

'I told you—I asked him not to.'

There was an emptiness as he moved away from her and went back to his chair: a feeling of coldness, of loneliness. Kaitlin had to force herself to concentrate on the issue at hand.

'Why do I get the feeling there's also another reason why Bill didn't talk to me himself?'

'What do you think, Kaitlin?'

'Am I right?'

'Maybe.'

'What was it?' She threw the words at him. And when he remained silent, 'I need to know—don't you understand?'

'Bill Seally,' Flynn said deliberately, 'is a weak man.'

'No! You're wrong! Bill is sweet and gentle and kind.'

'I'm sure he's all of those things. Bill hates making

waves, he has a great need to be liked. He shies away from conflict, especially where friends are involved. A good friend's daughter, in your case.'

Kaitlin's cheeks were flushed. 'He would have got the money I owed him,' she said unhappily. 'I've always tried very hard to keep up my payments.'

'Not hard enough. You're in arrears.'

'I know that. But in the end Bill wouldn't have lost any money. I was always utterly determined to pay every cent, including interest on back payments.'

'How did you plan to do that?'

'Profits from the ranch. Things are starting to come right, Flynn. Slowly, I admit, but it's happening. It's been an uphill battle ever since Dad died, but I'm hoping my financial situation will improve.'

'You can't blame Bill for having some doubts.'

The flush in Kaitlin's face deepened. 'If he felt that way, why didn't he say anything? We could have talked. Bill knew how things were at the ranch. Knew that Dad had...' She bit her lip. 'He understood that I needed time.'

'How much time, Kaitlin?'

'I don't know exactly.'

'Bill didn't know either, and the situation was beginning to worry him.'

She shouldn't be surprised, Kaitlin realized. The signs had been there for some time, only she had been too preoccupied to notice them. There had been a strange restlessness in Bill and Alice, his wife, when she did see them, a way they had of not meeting her eyes when they talked. Bill and her father had been boyhood friends, classmates, their friendship was one of the few constants in her life. When her parents had died, Bill and Alice had been there, phoning her, extending invitations. Yet now that she came to think of it, she could not remember the last invitation: she had been too busy to wonder about it.

Kaitlin looked at Flynn. 'You may not believe me, but I didn't know about the mortgage until after my father's death.'

'I see.'

'Until then I'd had almost nothing to do with the running of the ranch.'

'No part in the finances?'

'None,' she admitted.

She would not tell Flynn, who seemed to be holding her destiny in those very competent-looking hands, of her dismay when she had sat in the office of her father's lawyer and learned that she had inherited the ranch. A hollow inheritance, for the ranch was so heavily in debt that it didn't belong to her in the true sense of the word. Apart from the ranch, there had been nothing else.

Helplessly she had looked across the desk at the lawyer. 'I don't understand... It seems impossible...'

'It's the way it is, Miss Mullins. I'm sorry.'

'I always thought we were secure. We lived well. There was money for parties and travelling and for college.'

'There was money once,' the lawyer agreed, 'but much of it was used for the wrong purposes. There was also a lot of debt.'

'What are you saying, Mr. Barclay? I need the truth.'

'Your parents were living way beyond their means. I often warned your father to be more careful, but he kept insisting that things were fine. The mortgage was never meant to be more than short-term assistance, he was certain things would come right.'

But her father had been killed when he had skidded off the road on his way back to the ranch one stormy night. His truck had been found in a ditch. Witnesses said the vehicle seemed to veer suddenly on a slippery section of the road, before rolling over onto its side. Kaitlin had pretended to accept the explanation, but privately she had wondered if grief over her mother's death had made her father careless. He had had no time to put his affairs in order.

Kaitlin looked at Flynn, shivering when she saw the enigmatic expression in his eyes, the implacability in the firm jaw. 'You're saying that Bill was eager to rid himself of the mortgage.'

'Correct.'

'That's when you appeared on the scene. Flynn Henderson to the rescue.'

Flynn shrugged, seemingly unconcerned by her sarcasm.

'Some coincidence that you just happened to come along at the right time,' Kaitlin went on grimly. 'Why don't I think that's the way it was?'

'Because you're too intelligent to believe it.'

He grinned at her, a grin that warmed his eyes and deepened the lines around them. If only, Kaitlin thought, he didn't have the ability to send her heart somersaulting in her chest.

'Then it wasn't coincidence.'

'Of course not. I've kept my eyes on the ranch ever since I left. I knew about the mortgage.'

'*How did you know?*'

'Wasn't difficult, Kaitlin. A person can make a point of knowing certain things. Besides, word gets around. When I thought Bill Seally was getting nervous I went to talk to him. To his credit, I had to speak to him several times before he made his decision.'

Despite the heat of the day, Kaitlin was feeling colder by the minute. 'Five years, and all that time you were just biding your time to take over here.'

That grin again. 'Five years ago all I had was a burning ambition. I knew what I wanted, but I couldn't afford to pay for a corner of one barn let alone the whole ranch.'

That was one thing that puzzled her: how on earth had Flynn managed to acquire what must surely be a small fortune?

Before she could ask the question, he said, 'Do you remember what I told you the last time we were together?'

'In the bar? You were with that red-haired woman. I think her name was Marietta.'

'So you remember that.' The eyes that held hers were unreadable.

'Sure, why not?' She strove to make her tone as casual and matter-of-fact as she could. Flynn did not have to know about the pain that knifed her at the very mention of the other woman's name.

'I think it's interesting that you would remember Marietta in such detail.' Still he held her gaze. 'But I wasn't referring to her. Kaitlin, do you remember what I said?'

'Why don't you jog my memory?'

'I promised you I'd be back for the ranch five years later. Five years to the day. I kept my promise, Kaitlin. Looking at your face, I know you never thought I would.'

Kaitlin felt the colour drain from her cheeks as she stared at the tall cowboy.

'So that's why you're here,' she said, when she could speak.

'Right.'

'You could have written. Or phoned.'

'I could have, I guess, but I decided to break it to you in person.'

'Without a thought to my feelings,' she accused unsteadily.

Flynn didn't answer, but there was an odd expression in the eyes that watched her.

Over the emotions that raged inside her, Kaitlin said, 'You knew I'd be shocked, but you wanted to see my face when you told me. What are you, Flynn—some kind of sadist?'

Flynn only shrugged.

Kaitlin's hands curled tightly against her sides. 'Anyway, now you've told me, you can go.'

'We have to talk, Kaitlin.'

'Not today, Flynn. Definitely not today. You have to give me time to think.'

For a long moment he looked down at her. Then, to her relief, he picked up his Stetson.

At the door of the house he turned. 'I'll be back.'

CHAPTER THREE

'HI, COWGIRL.'

Paintbrush in hand, the jeans-clad figure turned from the fence of the corral. 'Hi, yourself, cowboy.'

A week had passed since the last time he had seen her. 'You look busy, Kaitlin.'

Beneath the broad-brimmed Stetson, her eyes were intensely green, almost jade. 'You could say that. I didn't hear the plane this time, Flynn. Unless, of course, you reverted to your original mode of transport and arrived on horseback.'

He laughed. 'All the way from Austin? Hardly.' He glanced at the radio perched on a tree-stump beside the can of paint. 'Can't say I'm surprised you didn't hear the plane above the din.'

Kaitlin touched a dial and lowered the decibels. 'Not surprising at all,' she conceded as the throbbing beat of saxophone and drums faded into background music.

'You used to be a country and western fan, Kaitlin.'

'I still am, but there's nothing like variety. Been here long, Flynn?'

'A while.'

'I believe you've been watching me, cowboy.'

'You believe right.'

A few drops of white dropped from Kaitlin's brush as she leaned it across the rim of her bucket. As she came to Flynn, he was struck anew by her extreme slenderness and the gracefulness of her movements. Tendrils of hair escaped from beneath her Stetson to curl on her forehead, giving her a waiflike appearance that tugged at his heartstrings, and made his expression darken. The last thing Flynn wanted was for Kaitlin to touch his emotions.

'Why are you here?' she asked.

'To see you?' he suggested.

'Obviously—but not for friendly reasons. Whatever it is, it'll concern the ranch and the mortgage.'

'Does it have to be the reason? Men must come here all the time to woo the lovely Kaitlin Mullins.'

There was a sudden tightness around her lips. 'I don't have time for sarcasm, Flynn. Tell me why you're here, let's deal with it, whatever it is—and then I'll ask you to leave.'

A dark eyebrow lifted. 'Was I being sarcastic?'

'What do you call it?'

'I thought I was being complimentary. An invitation to one of your parties used to be quite an honour.'

A shadow seemed to pass briefly before Kaitlin's eyes. 'Is that what it was, Flynn?' Tension in her tone. 'Don't bother answering, because I don't want to hear it: not when what you call a compliment is really an insult.'

His eyes gleamed. 'Is that the way you feel about it? Had any parties lately?'

'No,' she said shortly.

'Really? You haven't told me about the men who visit you here.'

'There aren't any men.'

'I find that very hard to believe.'

'Believe whatever you like, Flynn.' Kaitlin pushed a hand through her hair, the gesture heavy with weariness. 'The truth is, I don't have time in my life for men. Just as I don't have time for wisecracks and insults and sarcasm.'

Flynn reached out and touched her left cheek, dabbing at it with his forefinger. As Kaitlin stepped abruptly backwards, he said mildly, 'Just removing some paint.'

'I'll wash it off at the house.'

He eyed her quizzically. 'When did you become so prickly, Kaitlin?'

'When did *you* become so overbearing and arrogant?' she countered.

For a long moment Flynn was silent, struck by the strain he saw in the delicate-featured face. Kaitlin looked ready to drop with fatigue, he thought.

Softly, he said, 'This kind of talk isn't really getting us anywhere, is it?'

'No... Which is why I wish you'd leave.'

'Not just yet,' he said evenly. 'For one thing, I want to know why you're out here slaving in this devilish heat.'

'Slaving? I'm just painting a fence, Flynn.'

'In this scorcher? You'll be telling me next that you enjoy working so hard when you could be somewhere cooler.'

Her lips quivered slightly. 'I do like painting.'

'You could be paying a man to do it for you.'

'Oh, for heaven's sake, Flynn, I can't believe you'd say anything so silly this close to the end of the twentieth century! Don't you know yet that a woman can do anything she puts her mind to?'

'Sure I do—but at risk of being labelled a chauvinist, I don't believe you took on this task just for the fun of it. So maybe you'd like to tell me why you're doing it?'

'Flynn—'

'And why you're working alone at it.'

Kaitlin took a shuddering breath. Hearing it, Flynn was overcome by a desire—an utterly insane desire—to rescue her from her drudgery, to protect her.

Protect her, indeed! Since when had spoiled Kaitlin Mullins—doted on by her parents, given everything she ever wanted—needed protection?

'Last time I was here, you told me you were shorthanded. Now I want to know whether you're trying to run the ranch on your own. The truth, Kaitlin.'

The look she threw him was part withering outrage, part assumed wide-eyed innocence. '*On my own*? Of course not! How could I possibly cope?'

'You couldn't,' Flynn acknowledged abruptly.

'There's your answer then.'

'No, because whatever you say, there don't seem to be many cowboys on this ranch.'

'Didn't we talk about that last time? There are cowboys—not many, but enough. If you haven't seen them it's because they're out on the range, roping and branding. So you see, Flynn, your concerns are unwarranted.'

Kaitlin accompanied the words with a grin which, if she

hadn't looked quite so tired, might have succeeded in being provocative. As it was, it made her look more vulnerable than ever.

Flynn swallowed down hard over the unwelcome and unexpected lump in his throat. 'All the same,' he said after a moment, 'I still wonder how you're managing.'

'Isn't it enough that I'm doing it?'

'How, Kaitlin?'

'I don't owe you any answers, Flynn.'

'I think you're forgetting something.'

'The mortgage.' Her eyes clouded. 'I haven't forgotten it. It haunts me day and night, I haven't stopped thinking about it since you told me about it. I know I have to make regular payments, and I will.'

'Glad to hear it.'

'Of course, I realize that with Bill out of the picture the whole scenario has changed. No matter what you say about Bill—and I keep wishing he'd had the courage to tell me the truth—he was never unkind.'

'Whereas you see me—' Flynn's grin was wicked '—as some kind of monster?'

'I get the feeling you've turned into an unforgiving sort of man.'

Flynn's grin vanished. Didn't Kaitlin understand that some things were impossible to forgive?

After a moment he said, 'I'm a businessman, Kaitlin. Unlike your good buddy Bill, I don't let friendship or personalities get in the way of my business arrangements. If that makes me unkind and a monster, then maybe that's what I am—at least in your eyes. Now, Kaitlin, suppose you tell me, honestly, why there are so few cowboys at the ranch.'

'I still say I don't have to give you any answers. As long as you get your payments, that's all that should interest you.'

'But I *am* interested.'

'Flynn...'

'*Why*, Kaitlin?'

'I don't know why you're pressing this when you know

the answer already.' Her voice was flat. 'Money—or the lack of it, Flynn. It's as simple as that.'

'You can't afford any cowboys?'

'I keep telling you there are some. Just not as many as there should be.'

'Which is why you're working flat-out yourself. A slip of a girl, taking on the work of a bunch of men.'

Two bright spots of red burned in Kaitlin's cheeks, and her eyes sparkled with anger. 'Is that pity I hear in your voice, Flynn Henderson? If it is, save it for someone else. The ranch is my life. I am where I want to be. Living the way I want to live. Sure, I admit things could be better, but they could be a lot worse, too. I'm coping. And if there's one thing I can't bear, it's pity. I'll manage, Flynn, somehow I'll manage.'

Flynn thought admiringly, and not for the first time, that Kaitlin had more guts and drive and independence than both her parents had possessed together.

He asked, 'What happened to the girl whose life was one mad whirl of fun? Horses, swimming, picnics, parties? What happened to her, Kaitlin?'

'Did she exist?' Kaitlin's tone was brittle.

'Don't you remember?'

'Dimly.'

'Whereas I remember her vividly. She was lovely, Kaitlin. Pretty beyond belief, with skin like roses just out of the bud. Vibrant, and so full of fun that you couldn't help being happy, too, when you were with her. And sexy, Kaitlin. So sexy that a man thought he'd go crazy if he couldn't make love to her.'

Kaitlin looked away from him, and then back. 'Are you sure she was real, Flynn?'

'Flesh and blood down to the last dainty toe. What happened to her?'

'I have no idea.'

'Think you could find her?'

'How can I, when she's gone?'

'Has she really gone, Kaitlin?'

'Forever. Never to return.' A small smile of wry amusement touched her lips. 'And maybe it's all for the best, Flynn—she sounds revolting.'

'Actually, she was delightful.'

Kaitlin swallowed. 'The fact is, she's gone, Flynn, and she's not about to return. That girl lived in another world, another era.' Picking up her paintbrush, she began to paint once more, slapping paint on the fence with what seemed to Flynn to be unnecessary energy.

A few minutes went by. Then Kaitlin said, 'Talking about the past, Flynn, I could ask you what happened to the guy I once knew. The young cowboy. He was fun, too, at least until—' She stopped abruptly.

'Until?' Flynn prompted.

'It doesn't matter.'

'Maybe it does to me.' His face was still, his tone urgent.

'It doesn't matter,' she said again.

'Until? The cowboy was fun *until what*, Kaitlin?'

She was working quickly now, her small oval face fierce with concentration. Briefly she turned to him. 'Don't press me, Flynn. That world, the one we lived in, has vanished. Forever. There's no way it can ever come back to life.'

'You're certain of that?'

'Positive. The person you talk of, I can't believe I was ever that girl, Flynn. If you must know, I wouldn't even want to be like her any more. As for you, I just have to look at you to know you could never be that sweet young cowboy again, either. So just drop the subject—OK?'

For a few minutes she worked in silence. Presently she turned to him. 'You still haven't told me why you're here, Flynn.'

'We'll talk about it later. When I've helped you with the fence.'

She stared at him. 'Oh no, I don't think so.'

'Where can I find a brush and another pot of paint?'

'It's out of the question, Flynn!'

'Two can do the job twice as quickly as one. Just think, Kaitlin, you'll be able to go back to the house earlier. Imagine yourself in the tub, and after a nice long soak, enjoying a cool drink.' He grinned at her.

Kaitlin hesitated a moment, her expression one of such

open yearning that Flynn understood quite how tempting his offer was.

'I don't think so,' she said at last, but her tone was reluctant.

'Why not?'

'Because I can't afford to pay you for your labour.'

'Did I say anything about charging?'

'It's obvious, isn't it? You keep telling me you're a businessman. What would you do, Flynn—add the painting costs to the mortgage?'

'Actually,' he drawled, 'just this once, my services won't cost you a cent. Where's a brush, Kaitlin? And don't try putting me off, because it won't work. Where's all your stuff? In the shed, where it used to be?'

A glance at Flynn's face must have convinced Kaitlin that he meant what he said, for after a moment she nodded. Minutes later he emerged from the shed, paintbrush in one hand, hammer and a screwdriver in the other: in case something needed repair, he explained.

For a while they painted in silence. Eventually, Flynn said, 'Time for a break.'

'You can take a break, Flynn. I won't.' Flynn, the weakling, her tone implied.

He was unabashed. 'Trying to prove something to me, or to yourself, Kaitlin?'

'I'm not proving anything to anybody. I'm just determined to get a job of work done.' Beneath her tan she was pale, and her eyes looked exhausted.

'Do you think a break would hold you up?' Flynn asked, quite gently.

'When there's so much left to do? Yes, it would hold me up.' Her tone was defiant.

There was no arguing with her when she was in this mood. 'Fine,' Flynn said easily, 'we'll go on in that case.'

Side by side, they worked, sharing the same can of white paint. Around them the air bristled with tension, but Flynn pretended not to notice it. He began to talk, light talk, inconsequential: a question about a cowboy he remembered from the past; a comment about an oil-strike which had been reported in the Texas newspapers recently; the weather. Little by little, the tension lessened.

They had moved to another section of fence when Kaitlin said, 'Remember when you roped the calf? I asked you if you'd been a rodeo rider?'

'I remember.'

'Were you on the rodeo circuit, Flynn?'

He looked at her. 'Yes.'

'After you left the ranch?'

'Yes again.'

Her eyes sparkled. 'So I was right! What did you do on the circuit, Flynn? Roping?'

'At first. Until I started riding the bulls.'

'*Bull-riding*?' She looked at him in disbelief. 'Is that a joke?'

'No.'

'It's so hard to imagine. Bull-riding! I'm not sure if you're having me on.'

He shot her a teasing glance. 'You don't think I'd be capable of it?'

Slowly, she said, 'I can picture you in the rodeos, Flynn. You were always great on a horse.'

'Glad you noticed,' he said drily.

'But the bulls! Bull-riding isn't your ordinary run-of-the-mill rodeo stunt. Daredevils go in for it.'

His grin was wicked. 'You didn't figure me for a daredevil?'

'The Flynn I knew five years ago wasn't. What made you do it? Fame? Glory?'

His eyes sparkled. 'How about fun? Challenge?'

'*Fun*? You rode the bulls for fun?'

'The money was tempting,' he admitted.

'I know you can make money on the rodeo circuit, if you're good.'

'Which I was, I guess. And, yes, I won a lot.' Flynn made no attempt at modesty. 'And you're right, Kaitlin, when you knew me I wasn't your typical bull-rider. I was content with a comfortable routine, working on the ranch, enjoying the only life I could imagine. But do you know, once I started in the rodeos, I was hooked. Couldn't stop.

There was always more challenge, more fun. More prize money.'

'Men get killed riding the bulls,' Kaitlin said flatly.

'Some do.' Flynn shrugged. 'But I'm here, alive to tell the tale. And there were compensations.'

Kaitlin was quiet awhile. Flynn watched her working, applying paint to the fence with long even brushstrokes.

'What compensations?' she asked at last, 'apart from fun and money?'

'The other cowboys respect you. As for the women, they adore you.'

'You'd enjoy that,' Kaitlin said brittly.

'What normal red-blooded man would object to women throwing themselves at him? The groupies of the rodeo circuit. That's how I met Elise.'

Kaitlin's hands stilled. 'Elise?'

'My wife. She used to hang around the arenas. We got talking, went out together. Perhaps I drank too much one night. At any rate, I found myself the next day with a hangover, a marriage licence and a wife.'

In a level voice, Kaitlin said, 'But you must have loved her—surely?'

Flynn was silent a moment as he tried to bring the face of his ex-wife into his mind, and found that he couldn't. And that was surprising, because he'd never had any trouble picturing Kaitlin, despite all the time that had gone by since he'd last seen her.

Elise… Good figure, pretty enough face, though a bit coarse. A mouth like a cowboy or a sailor. At first her crudities had amused him, but after a while he had found himself repelled by the things she'd said. Sexy? Yes. Always ready to lure a man into bed—and not only her husband, as Flynn had discovered one memorable day when he had returned home at a time when she wasn't expecting him. Flynn had thrown the other man's clothing out of the window and watched him scramble naked from the house, with just a bath-towel around him to protect his honour. Then he had ordered Elise to leave.

'The marriage is over. Things didn't work out. I told you that the other day,' he said.

'I know. But once... You must have loved Elise. Didn't you, Flynn?'

Kaitlin's tone was so odd: Flynn wished he knew why that was.

Harshly, he said, 'Love? Heck, I don't know. If you're talking sexual attraction, sure, I was attracted. But love? I don't think I know what love is.'

'You're a bitter man, Flynn,' Kaitlin said slowly.

He shrugged. 'I prefer to call it realistic.'

'Have you seen Elise since you split up?'

'Not since the divorce was made final.'

'I see... Was she... Was she pretty?' Kaitlin asked. A second later, she said, very quickly, 'Forget I said that.'

'She was pretty.' Flynn searched Kaitlin's face for reaction, but her eyes were turned away from his, so he couldn't see their expression.

At last he said, 'Anything else you want to know about Elise?'

'Not particularly. But there is something I do want to know, and it doesn't concern your love-life or your ex-wife.' This time her gaze was firm and direct. 'How did you manage to afford the mortgage?'

Flynn laughed. 'How did the simple cowboy come by so much cash? You took your time asking the question, I've been waiting for it.'

Her face was flushed. 'I didn't put it so crudely.'

'You didn't have to, it meant the same—didn't it? It's the question your parents would have wanted answered, as well.'

Kaitlin's gaze was clear and green-eyed and steady. 'In the circumstances, the question isn't unreasonable.'

'I guess not.'

'You made all that money on the rodeo circuit, Flynn?'

'No, Kaitlin, rodeos don't pay *that* well. But it was a start. I was on a roll, winning more than the others. Naturally, I knew it couldn't last. Like you, Kaitlin, I'm aware that bull-riding can kill a man. You can be as good as you like, but sooner or later you forget to concentrate, you make a mistake, and the smallest mistake can cost you your life. The brute gores you, or stamps on your chest. I decided to get out before that happened. By then I had a tidy little sum put away in the bank. But I needed more. So I looked around for an investment. Came across one just when I needed it.'

'What kind of investment, Flynn?' Kaitlin was making no effort to hide her fascination.

'Oil.'

'*Oil*?'

Flynn laughed at her amazement. 'Cowboys do know about the black stuff that hides in the bowels of the earth. I met a man, Kaitlin. He told me about an oilfield that was struggling, in dire need of financial aid. A tiny field, not big enough to lure the big guys. Investors were needed, no matter how small. I went out to look at the field. Nothing much to see, and I didn't know much about oil anyway, but I happened to believe in the people running the place. So I put in my money. The outfit did well, wildly surpassing all our expectations. The payback was bigger than anything I ever imagined.'

'Making you rich enough to take over my mortgage.'

'You got it.' Flynn nodded.

Kaitlin's look was suddenly fierce. 'I still don't understand. You couldn't have known things would turn out the way they did. Mum dying, and then Dad.'

'I didn't foresee that—how could I? I told you that last time I was here—remember? But there were things I did know. Your father had started to drink. His management of the ranch left much to be desired; inexperienced as I was five years ago, I was aware of that. It was just a matter of time before things deteriorated to the point where he wouldn't be able to continue.'

Kaitlin's head jerked up. 'You couldn't have known that!'

'I did,' Flynn said calmly. 'I planned to make your father an offer, one he couldn't refuse.'

'He would never have let you have his ranch, Flynn.'

'We'll never know that, will we?' he said calmly, 'but I believe he would.'

Green eyes were furious. 'So you laid your plans right

from the start. Made money on the rodeos. Invested wisely.
Waited till the time was right to come back.'

'Five years to the day. Just as I promised.'

The slender figure was galvanized into sudden movement. Swinging the arm holding the paintbrush, she said,
'Get out, Flynn! Off this ranch.' And when he did not
move, but merely stroked another swath of paint along a
fence-post, 'Didn't you hear me? You're not welcome
here.'

Drily, Flynn said, 'You made your point in your first
sentence, the rest is overkill. And if you don't want white
ground, be careful with that paintbrush.'

'You are insufferable,' Kaitlin hissed. 'Overbearing, autocratic, and a darn sight too sure of yourself.'

God, but she was gorgeous when she was angry! Green
eyes blazing, cheeks red, every inch of her sexy little body
vibrant with furious energy. Flynn ached to pull Kaitlin into
his arms, to cover her with kisses—but this was not the
moment. The fact that he had never once been so attracted
to the deliberately provocative Elise—or any other of the
many women who'd made no secret of their attraction to
him—gave him no joy.

In a hard voice he said, 'Any other adjectives you can
come up with?'

'A few. Not as polite.'

'Try me, Kaitlin.'

'No.' As if to calm herself, she took a deep breath. 'You
know what I think of you. Additional adjectives wouldn't
make the slightest difference. I want you to go, Flynn.'

'You're wasting your breath, Kaitlin.'

'I know you own the mortgage, and at the moment I
can't do anything about that. But you don't own the ranch.'

'Correct.'

'You're going to want payment.'

'Correct again.'

'You'll get it. I'll make sure of that.'

'Glad to hear it—for your sake.'

Beside him, he heard a little hiss of breath. 'Are you
saying you'd foreclose on the mortgage if I don't pay?'

'I knew I didn't have to put it into words.'

Kaitlin looked shaken. 'I'll see you get paid—somehow. That doesn't change the fact that we can do business without seeing each other.'

'Suppose *I* want to see *you*.'

Kaitlin hesitated, as if she wondered what he meant by the remark. After a moment, she shook her head. 'No. We can communicate by letter or phone. You're not welcome here, Flynn.'

'I'm sorry,' he said, in a voice which made it clear that he wasn't sorry at all.

'You weren't always so thick-skinned, Flynn.'

'Maybe not. Look, Kaitlin, it's hot and you're wasting your breath. You can call me every rude word in your vocabulary, but it won't make any difference—I'm not ready to leave just yet.'

'I'm sure you know you're annoying me.'

'Poor Kaitlin.' He grinned at her before dipping his brush in the paint. 'Say, cowgirl, do you really mean to finish the fence today?'

'Of course.'

'There's always tomorrow.'

'I have other things to do then.'

'It's very hot out here.'

'Do you know how often you've said that? If you've had enough for now, Flynn, you can call it quits.'

'Will you join me?'

'No.' Kaitlin's tone was flat. 'I'll finish the fence, if it kills me.'

The angry flush had left her cheeks. With the colour gone, she was looking more exhausted than ever. Something wrenched deep inside Flynn at the sight of the small, pale, weary face. 'It very well may kill you,' he said gruffly. 'That may be the price you'll pay for your stubbornness.'

'I'm tougher than you think, Flynn.'

'Are you, Kaitlin? Are you really?'

'Yes. So why don't you go and rest in the shade, cowboy, while I get on with my work?'

Flynn merely grinned at the sarcasm. For a while they worked in silence. The noonday sun was fiercer than ever, the heat merciless. Even the cattle on the range would be taking shelter if they could find any shade.

Flynn worked with effortless ease. Kaitlin, he noticed, was having more difficulty. Huge beads of sweat were bunched on her upper lip and her forehead, and her T-shirt was damp. Now and then her paintbrush hovered unsteadily over a fence-post, and her brushstrokes were becoming erratic. Flynn didn't suggest again that she take a break—he knew only too well the response such a suggestion would elicit—but he watched her closely.

When the paintbrush dropped out of Kaitlin's hand, Flynn's head jerked up. When she swayed, he moved quickly, catching her as her body was about to touch the ground.

For a few seconds she lay, inert in his arms, her eyes closed. He was gathering her closer, lifting her off her feet, when her eyes snapped open.

'No,' she said weakly.

'You need help.'

'I'm fine.'

'You're anything but fine, Kaitlin.'

'Just a bit dizzy for a moment. Put me down, Flynn.'

'Don't be a bloody idiot.'

'I'm fine,' she persisted, 'really I am. Put me down, Flynn.'

'You need to be someplace cool.'

'Later. I... I have to finish the fence first.'

'No, Kaitlin. You've proved you're strong and determined, but there's no point in giving yourself sunstroke. Only a fool would do that.'

She was still protesting, though weakly, as he carried her towards the ranch-house.

'At least, put me down,' she pleaded, pushing her hand against his chest.

'No.'

'I'm too heavy to carry all the way.'

'You're as light as a baby,' he informed her abruptly. 'Don't you ever stop to eat?'

On the horse a few days earlier, with his arms around her, Flynn had been aware of Kaitlin's fragility. Now, as he cradled her in his arms, he was shocked by how little she weighed.

But that was where all comparison with a baby ended. The girl in Flynn's arms was all woman: soft and sweet despite her extreme slenderness. Kaitlin was so sexy that she could drive a man right out of his mind without even trying.

At the same time, she made that same man yearn to cherish her and keep her free from all harm. Longings he had already experienced, and hated to feel again now. Flynn did not want to feel protective, certainly not towards stubborn, snobbish, callous Kaitlin Mullins.

His lips were set in a hard line as he pushed open the unlocked door of the ranch-house. Kaitlin made an attempt to stand upright, but his arms were rock-hard around her, keeping her fragile body wedged firmly against his.

'You can put me down now,' she said again.

'What's your hurry?' he asked roughly.

'You know I don't want you carrying me.'

'Tough.'

'Anyway... We're inside now. Flynn... Flynn, where are you going?'

'Your bedroom.'

He wondered if he imagined the sudden jerking movement of her body against his.

'No!' she said.

Flynn ignored the protest. Without stopping, he walked through the front of the house, and down the hallway. Five years had not dulled his memory, he knew very well which room was Kaitlin's. Within seconds he had put her down on the bed.

Looking around him, Flynn saw that nothing had changed. The room was as he remembered it: pink and white drapes and a deep rose carpet; a shelf of small stuffed animals, given to Kaitlin at various stages of her childhood and never discarded. A bed with brass railings, covered with cushions in a variety of colours and fabrics. An intensely feminine room, totally at variance with the prickly woman who inhabited it.

'Which is the real Kaitlin?' he asked abruptly.

'I don't understand.'

'The soft feminine girl, or the stubborn, independent woman?'

Her gaze met his. 'What do *you* think, Flynn?' Mixed with the fatigue shading the lovely green eyes, was a glimmer of amusement.

'A bit of both?' Flynn suggested. 'Am I right?'

'Why don't *you* answer the question?' she asked provocatively.

Rosebud lips parted in a smile, revealing even white teeth and the tip of a small pink tongue. Without thinking, Flynn bent down. Beneath his lips, he felt Kaitlin shudder. He was quite still for a long moment, savouring the feel of her warm mouth against his, tasting the moist sweetness where her lips were slightly parted. He could have stayed forever just like this.

His arms slid beneath her, lifting her against him, feeling her breasts against his throat. Once more memory stirred, as well as an intense emotion which he did not want to experience. Involuntarily, he groaned. His tongue touched her lips, he was about to explore her mouth, to experience delights which had for so long been denied him.

And then he remembered why he was here, in her bedroom, at the ranch. And he sat up.

'Why?' Kaitlin asked. Her eyes, usually so green, were smoky now, and slightly unfocused.

'Why did I kiss you?' Flynn forced a shrug. 'I guess I felt like it.'

'Why did you stop?'

The unexpected question sent heat flooding into his loins. *Because if I hadn't stopped, I wouldn't have stopped at all.* That was the answer he could have given her: it would have been the truth.

'The first day we ever met,' he said roughly, 'you asked me if I was going to kiss you.'

'I haven't forgotten.'

'We were side by side on our horses, both of us aching to get closer.'

'You were scared of my father's reaction.'

'I kissed you, Kaitlin.'

'I remember that, too.'

'But this time I've stopped.'

The eyes that held his were still dazed. The lips, which just moments earlier had tasted so sweet, were trembling. Flynn was rocked by a tremor of emotion. But there were things he knew about Kaitlin Mullins. He told himself to ignore the temptation to believe that she had changed, to remember instead that she was a little tease, who only cared about herself.

'Why did I stop?' Now his tone was derisive. 'Same answer—I felt like it.'

Kaitlin was so close to him that he could hear the hiss rise in her throat. 'You're a rotten swine, Flynn! I used to think I knew you—obviously I was wrong.'

Flynn's laughter was short and humourless. 'Perhaps we were both wrong in our opinions of each other. How do you feel?'

'Swell. Ready to go back to the fence.'

'You'll be a damn little fool if you do.'

'There's nothing wrong with me. OK, so I was a bit weak for a moment. One little moment, Flynn. I'd have been perfectly all right if you hadn't chosen to play the strong macho guy. I intend finishing the fence today.'

She sat up, but he seized her shoulders and forced her back against the pillows.

'Lie still, Kaitlin. Don't you dare move till I get back.'

'Bossy, aren't you?' Her tone was saucy, but she looked very tired.

'Better believe it,' he told her as he walked out of the room. He was back a few minutes later, a damp cloth in one hand, a cup in the other.

'What on earth…' Kaitlin struggled to sit once more, as he put the cool wet cloth to her forehead.

'Lie still,' he ordered.

After a moment, she did as he ordered. Her eyes closed as he held the cloth in place, and he was able to study her unobserved: the long eyelashes fringing the tops of her cheeks; the lovely soft hair, loosened from the pony-tail and spilling over the pillow; the lips curving at the corners and trembling just a little—how he *yearned* to kiss them again; the pulse beating in the hollow of the slender throat; and the rise and fall of small breasts, nipples clearly visible beneath the damp clinging fabric of her T-shirt.

Despite her show of toughness, Kaitlin looked more vulnerable than ever.

'How does it feel?' he asked.

'Good.'

'That's it?'

'Very good, actually.' She sighed.

He laughed. 'If it's so good, why the sigh?'

'I was just thinking, it's been a long time since anyone did anything like this. Something personal, just for me.'

The wrenching inside him was becoming unpleasantly familiar. 'No family, Kaitlin?'

'How can there be—now?'

'I'm not talking about your parents, I know they're gone. But is there no one else? Other relatives? Friends? How about Bill Seally and his wife?'

'No relatives, apart from a few aunts and uncles who barely know me. As for Bill and Anne, they're in Austin.'

'There must be somebody,' Flynn persisted. 'That party you gave. All those people.'

Beneath his fingers she grew very still. 'I didn't think you'd remember the party.'

'I remember,' he said grimly. 'A house full of guests.'

'You weren't there, Flynn, so how would you know?' Her tone was flat.

Was this the moment to talk? No, he decided. He was in no mood to be patronised or humiliated. Besides, there was no advantage to be gained from talking: the past was over and done with.

Voice hard, he said, 'The point is, aren't any of those people able to help you now?'

'No.'

'Poor Kaitlin.'

She must have caught the mockery in his tone, for she sat up and pushed his hand away. 'Not poor Kaitlin at all,' she told him briskly. 'Must be weakness that made me sound sorry for myself. Fact is, I don't *need* anyone. And that goes for you, too, Flynn. Thanks for helping me, but you've done your bit—you can go now.'

He had been right, Flynn thought, not to bring up what had happened on that night five years earlier. Kaitlin would have made short shrift of anything he might have said.

Instead he said, 'Nothing like gratitude to make a man feel good and wanted. I brought you some tea, Kaitlin. Two spoons of sugar in it.'

'I don't take sugar.'

'It'll give you some energy. Drink up, cowgirl.'

'You're awfully bossy, Flynn, but I've already told you that. If I drink, will you go?'

'When we've talked.'

Kaitlin drank slowly. Most of the colour had returned to her face, Flynn saw. She no longer looked as if she was about to faint. Neither, however, did she look particularly robust.

When she had finished the tea, she put down the cup and looked at Flynn. 'I know why you're here. Doesn't take a genius to have figured it out. It's about the mortgage.'

'Not exactly.'

She looked surprised. 'What then?'

Leaning forward, Flynn cupped a small pointed chin in his hand. Against the roughness of his palm, Kaitlin's skin felt soft and delicate. Quietly, he asked, 'Why was it so important to paint the whole fence today?'

Kaitlin's eyes did not meet his as she shrugged. 'Once I've started a chore, I like to finish it.'

'Or perhaps,' Flynn suggested, 'you needed to get it done today because there are a hundred other things that need doing tomorrow.'

Kaitlin moved in her seat. 'You know about ranches, Flynn, there's always work to be done.'

'Sure. And there should be enough people to do it. So I ask you again, Kaitlin—why?'

'You know the reason—I can't afford to pay more in wages than I'm paying already. You've known all along.' Her tone was defiant. 'Why all the questions, Flynn? Do you want to see me squirm? Well, I won't. I may be hard up, but I don't squirm. Not for you, not for anybody.'

'You'll just keep working yourself to the bone.'

'There's no alternative,' she said, still in that same defiant tone. 'But to get back to my payments, you don't have to worry—you'll get whatever's owing.'

Flynn studied the feisty girl who was like no other woman he had ever known. 'There is an alternative,' he said quietly.

Her eyes shone with sudden hope. 'Oh?'

'Sell me the ranch.'

In an instant, her dizziness apparently forgotten, Kaitlin had shot up and was on her feet. 'You're kidding, aren't you?'

'Did it sound as if I was?'

The lovely eyes flashed with fire. 'The ranch isn't for sale.'

'You haven't heard my offer yet,' Flynn drawled. Then he named a figure.

Just for a moment something came and went in Kaitlin's eyes, as if, thought the watching man, she was both amazed and very tempted. Then she shook her head. 'No, Flynn.'

'You haven't given yourself time to consider the offer.'

'I don't have to,' she said unsteadily. 'I love the ranch. It's my home, my parents' home. I can't just give it up.'

'There's more to the offer, Kaitlin.'

'What else could there be?'

His eyes held hers steadily. 'This can still be your home.'

She looked confused now. 'I don't understand. Are you offering me a job?'

'I'm asking you to marry me.'

Once more emotion showed in her face, emotion of the most intense kind; it was in her eyes, in the sudden trembling of her lips. Flynn held his breath as he waited for her to speak.

But when she did so, her voice was contemptuous. '*Marry*? *You*?'

In that moment there was the sound of her mother in Kaitlin's tone, the sound of that well-bred Southern beauty in whose eyes Flynn Henderson had never been, could never be, anything more than a simple cowboy.

'Why not?' he asked mockingly.

'Give me one reason why I should.'

'You'd still have your home.'

'And you, Flynn? What would you have?'

He looked at her, wondering why it was that of all the women he had met over the years, Kaitlin Mullins was still the sexiest, the most desirable. She had entered his blood five years ago, and he knew now that she had never left it. None of which he was about to tell her. Kaitlin Mullins had hurt him badly, and he wasn't ready to forgive her. Maybe he never would be.

'I'd have a wife,' he told her flatly.

'Why do you need a wife, Flynn?'

He shrugged. 'You're imaginative, Kaitlin—why don't you tell me?'

Her eyes sparkled with challenge. 'Convenience?' She threw the word at him. 'Someone to cook your meals and make certain your clothes are washed and ironed and mended. A hostess who'll plan parties for all those oilmen and their wives.'

'Anything else you can come up with?'

'Sure—someone to fill that empty space left by Elise.'

Flynn laughed. 'You seem to have thought of everything.'

'Everything except...' Kaitlin stopped abruptly.

'Except?' he prompted.

Her face was flushed suddenly. 'It doesn't matter.'

'You were starting to say something, Kaitlin. What was it?'

'It doesn't matter,' she said again. 'Besides, I know the answer already.'

'Do you?'

'Yes. You see, there's something I just realized. I know why you want me.'

'You're a mind-reader?' he drawled.

'I don't have to be. That promise you made to yourself, that you'd come back to claim the ranch...'

He waited tensely. 'What about it?'

'I have a feeling there was more to it.'

'Whatever it is you're trying to say, why don't you just say it, Kaitlin?'

'Did your promise also include a claim to the daughter of the ranch?'

He looked down at her a long moment, noticing the anger in the lovely green eyes, the tautness around the kissable lips.

'Flynn?' she demanded.

He decided to let her have it straight. 'You've guessed it.'

He saw her flinch, and her cheeks paled a little. 'At least you're admitting it.'

'No reason not to.'

'Except that you didn't mention it at the time.'

'I didn't,' he told her insolently, 'think of it at the time. That part of the promise only came later: after I'd already left the ranch, after my marriage to Elise.'

'Why, Flynn? Why?' And when he remained silent, 'Because of some grudge?'

She was looking at him as if, for the life of her, she had no idea what it was all about.

Flynn shrugged. 'The reason isn't important.'

'Don't you have any shame, Flynn?'

He grinned at her. 'None. In fact, it was the promise that reminded me of my plans, that kept me going when times were rough.'

'I see.' Kaitlin seemed to have recovered from the worst of the shock: her shoulders were straight, her chin high. 'You laid your plans well, Flynn. Made lots of money. Kept an eye on the ranch. Waited for the right moment to pounce. But in the end you miscalculated.'

'If I believed that, I wouldn't have come here.'

'You may as well believe it, Flynn. If you want to own a ranch, look for some other place. This particular ranch isn't up for grabs.'

She paused a moment. When she went on, her tone had acquired an extra firmness. 'And I'm not up for grabs, either.'

Harshly, Flynn said, 'I suggest you think carefully before you say no, Kaitlin.'

'I've done all the thinking I need, Flynn. Now I want

you to get off my land. You're not welcome here. You may as well know, I can't stand the sight of you.'

'That wasn't always the case,' he said derisively. 'Why don't you think about *that*, Kaitlin, tonight, when you're all alone in your narrow little bed?'

Kaitlin didn't wait until the night. As she stood at the window of her bedroom and watched Flynn's plane rise in the sky, the memories came unbidden: memories that were as fresh and as vivid as if the events they represented had only just taken place.

CHAPTER FOUR

'GOING to the stables, Katie?'

Kaitlin smiled eagerly at her mother. 'It seems like ages since I was on Star's back. The holiday was fantastic, Mom, but that's one good thing about returning to the ranch—apart from seeing you and Dad, of course—I can't wait to go riding.'

'Not alone, Katie.'

Halfway out of the kitchen door, Kaitlin stopped and looked at her mother in amazement. 'What are you saying, Mom? I've been riding the range by myself for as long as I can remember.'

'I know that, honey, but right now it's not safe for you to go out alone. We've had a bit of cattle thieving.'

'Why didn't you say anything about it before? Daddy didn't mention it, either.'

'All the excitement of seeing you back home, I guess, and it's almost two weeks since it happened. We'd have told you sooner or later.'

'Two weeks, Mom—that makes it ancient history.'

'Maybe, and we hope they won't come back. Still, we'd be a lot happier if you didn't go roaming around by yourself for a while. Wait until your father gets back from town.'

'That could be ages, and I was hoping to ride now.'

Her mother looked at her thoughtfully. 'Why don't you ask one of the cowboys to go with you? I'm sure the man working in the stables would oblige.'

Kaitlin thought of Harry, old and grizzled and inclined to be grumpy. The idea of having Harry as an escort, telling her to slow down when she was dying to race through the brushlands, was intolerable.

'It's either that or waiting for Dad,' said her mother.

'If I have to...'

Privately, Kaitlin sometimes thought her parents were far too concerned about her well-being, that they fussed for no cause. At the same time, she loved them dearly, and though she rebelled against them occasionally, by and large she lived in harmony with them.

'Your hat,' reminded her mother as she was about to leave the house.

'Don't worry, I'll wear my Stetson.'

'And your hands, Katie. Don't forget your gloves.'

'Oh, Mom,' Kaitlin sighed, knowing what was coming: she had heard the speech a thousand times.

'A lady should have beautiful hands, Katie. Soft and smooth and unfreckled.' Kaitlin's mother looked at her own immaculately groomed hands. 'I hope you're using your lotion morning and night.'

'Oh, Mom, Mom. You want so much for me to be a genteel lady, just like you were when you met Dad.'

'It's what I do want for you, Katie.'

'But I'm not like you, Mom. I'm a ranch-girl. A born and bred Texas ranch-girl. You've never been overly keen on horses, whereas I could happily spend my entire life riding the range.'

It was her mother's turn to sigh. 'Katie, my wild and wonderful Katie. I want so much for you, my darling. A beautiful home, a comfortable life. Above all, the right kind of husband.'

'I'm not a heroine in some Victorian novel,' Kaitlin said, impatience creeping into her voice.

'Of course, you're not. But don't discount what I'm saying, honey. Go riding with the cowboy, but wear your hat and gloves.'

'Mom…'

'You've just turned eighteen, Katie, and you think I fuss too much. But one day, when you're older, and your skin is still soft and lovely, you'll be glad you listened to me.'

Swinging her hat and gloves in one hand, holding a few carrots in the other, Kaitlin left the house. As she approached the stables, a host of familiar smells and sounds washed over her. She had spent two months away from the ranch and had enjoyed every day of her holiday: it was only when she saw her beloved horses that she realized quite how glad she was to be back home.

Kaitlin's horse, Star, greeted her with a whinny.

'Star, darling Star, how I missed you!' Kaitlin let the horse take the carrots from her hand. Then she stroked the glossy flanks and nuzzled her mouth against the horse's face.

When she'd saddled Star, Kaitlin went looking for Harry. She saw him at one end of the corral, his back to her, working with a foal.

'Harry!' she called.

No immediate response. But when she called again, he turned. The sun was behind him, so that she could not see his face, but there was something different about Harry. He seemed taller, more vital and athletic than Kaitlin remembered. Had the elderly cowboy been on a fitness kick of some kind, Kaitlin wondered.

'I'm back,' she called across the corral.

The cowboy came towards her, and his walk was the loose, lithe gait of a young man.

'Harry!' Kaitlin exclaimed. 'You've shed twenty years in two months. How could you…'

Her words trailed away as the cowboy came closer still. A shiver ran through her as she said, 'You're not Harry.'

The stranger pushed his Stetson backwards on his head. 'Reckon I'm not.'

Eyes, dark as the night, sparkled as the cowboy laughed down at her out of a face that was the most handsome Kaitlin had ever seen. Between wide shoulders, a muscled chest tapered to slender hips and impossibly long legs. At the most he was twenty-four years old.

Bemused, Kaitlin stared up at him. 'You're new here. I don't know you.'

'My name is Flynn.'

'Flynn…?'

'Flynn Henderson.' His voice was low, yet vibrant.

'And I'm Kaitlin. Kaitlin Mullins.'

'I know who you are.'

'You do?' Shock was robbing her of the ability to think clearly.

'You're the boss's daughter.'

'That's right.' She couldn't have said why she was suddenly defensive. 'I guess you've heard about me from the other cowboys?'

In the dark eyes, the sparkle intensified. 'Sure have.'

'What have you heard, Flynn Henderson?'

'That you've been away from the ranch awhile. Holiday of some sort?'

'Two months in Florida. I was at the coast with friends. A high-school graduation gift from my parents.'

'Have a nice time?'

'Fantastic. Two months of white sand and ocean. Picnics, dancing. Can you imagine anything more perfect?'

'Can't say since I've never had the time for beaches and picnics.' No hint of apology or self-defence in his tone, just a simple statement of fact.

'What else have you heard about me?' Kaitlin asked after a moment.

'That you're pretty. More than pretty, actually.'

'Thank you.' Kaitlin was used to compliments, yet for some reason she couldn't prevent a flush of pleasure.

'Of course,' he said, 'prettiness is in the eyes of the person doing the looking.'

'Meaning you don't agree with the other cowboys?'

'You're the prettiest girl I've seen in a long while.'

'Well.' The flush intensified. 'Have you heard anything else?'

'Sure have.'

'What?' Kaitlin asked, preparing herself to receive another compliment.

The cowboy grinned at her. 'They say you're a girl to be reckoned with.'

'In what way?'

'Sure you want to know?'

She kept her tone cool. 'Why not?'

'OK, then. The guys say you're spoiled. Anything you want, your adoring parents give you.'

Kaitlin forgot to be cool. 'That isn't true!' she burst out.

'That's not all I've heard.'

'What else is there?' she demanded.

'They say you're headstrong. Independent. Fond of your own way.' He grinned at her. 'Are they right?'

A momentary indignation vanished as humour took over. Kaitlin shot Flynn a dancing look. 'You don't really expect me to answer that. If you want to know what I'm like, you'll have to make up your own mind.'

'Look forward to it. I'd like to get to know you better.'

His words sent Kaitlin's heart spinning in an unexpected somersault. This was something that had never happened to her before: not with the boys from neighbouring ranches, nor with any of the young men she'd flirted with in Florida.

'You'll be able to get to know me now,' she said.

'Is that so?'

'Yes, since you're going to be riding with me.'

'Says who?' Flynn looked neither impressed by the honour, nor intimidated by Kaitlin's show of authority.

'I do.' And when he shot her an insolent grin, 'Not by my choice, Flynn Henderson. Actually, I prefer to ride alone.'

'Who's stopping you?'

'My parents. Seems there's been a bit of cattle-thieving around here.'

'Couple of weeks ago, right, but that's been taken care of.'

'Still, my parents think it's better if I don't ride the range alone. That's why you're to ride with me.' Something made her add, 'Not that *I'm* frightened. Personally, I think they're probably being a bit overprotective.'

'I see,' Flynn said, so calmly that Kaitlin was stung.

'You don't seem too pleased.'

'Guess I'm not.'

Oh, but this very handsome cowboy was sure of himself. Kaitlin tried to hide her anger. 'Did you have other plans?'

'After finishing with the foal, I was aiming to head for the west section, to help with the round-up.'

'I thought you wanted to get to know me.'

Once again the dark eyes sparkled. 'In my own time, yes. I didn't have any baby-sitting planned for this morning, Miss Mullins.'

Handsome or not, the cowboy had some nerve, and Kaitlin was not willing to put up with it.

'*Baby-sitting*! How dare you insult me like that?' Without thinking, she lifted her hand, swinging it in the direction of his face.

In a second, Flynn had caught the hand and forced it down to her side. 'Don't,' he ordered, quite calmly. 'You may be very pretty, and the boss's daughter to boot, but you don't get away with hitting me. Nobody does.'

Kaitlin forced herself to take a long calming breath. 'Sorry, I don't know what made me do that, I've never hit anyone before.'

'Why start with me?'

She couldn't tell him that his rejection of her had hurt. Avoiding the question, she said instead, 'Look, I don't want to ride with you any more than you want to ride with me.'

'Actually, I do want to ride with you,' he amazed her by saying. 'How about later? When I get back from the round-up?'

So it was going to be a battle of wills, one which Kaitlin had every intention of winning.

'I'm going out now,' she informed him. 'With or without you.'

'You're forgetting your parents' orders.'

'Not orders exactly, more like a request. As you say, the thieving's been taken care of, so there's no danger I'd come to any harm if I rode alone. Why would you care, anyway?'

'Your father is my boss, that's why.'

'And you're scared of him,' Kaitlin taunted, mortified that the handsome cowboy was treating her with such disdain.

'I'm not scared of him, but he does sign the pay-cheques. OK, Miss Mullins, since you're determined to go riding, I'll accompany you. Which way were you thinking of riding?'

'The north section.' Kaitlin gestured.

'You'll have to give me a few minutes.'

'Why?'

'Have to get the foal back to the stables, and saddle a horse for myself.'

Kaitlin watched, enraged, as Flynn went back to the foal. At the same time, she was also very excited, and warm with a longing she did not quite understand. A longing that was new to her, and which she didn't want to feel; not when it related to the cowboy who was treating her with such insolence.

She was spoiled, was she? Fond of getting her own way? Well, she would show that nervy Flynn Henderson just how skilled she was at doing just that.

He was leading a horse out of the stables, when she put her heels to the sides of her own horse. It might not take the disrespectful cowboy long to catch up with her, but in the meanwhile, she intended to put between them all the distance she could.

Star went easily from a trot to a canter to a gallop. Kaitlin laughed as the wind tugged at her hair, and the wild grasses of the prairies fell away beneath Star's hooves. Florida had been fun, but Kaitlin was back where she belonged, on the prairies, on the range, surrounded by cattle and horses and vast tracts of space.

She had not been riding long when she heard her name being called some distance behind her. '*Kaitlin*! *Kaitlin, wait*!' She rode even faster, only to gasp when a tall black horse shot past her, then wheeled and stopped in front of her on the narrow track.

Kaitlin exclaimed with anger as her horse reared. But, expert horsewoman that she was, it was only a minute before she was in control once more.

'I could have been thrown!' She flung the words at Flynn, when she was able to speak once more.

'I knew you wouldn't be. Not a little hellion like you. You look as if you were born to ride.' He was laughing at her.

'What in hell did you think you were doing?'

'What did you think *you* were doing?' he countered.

For a long moment she could only stare wordlessly at the tall cowboy who was far sexier than she had dreamed a man could be. The wind had flung his dark hair back from his forehead, despite his anger his eyes sparkled, and his teeth were very white against his tan.

The strange longing she had felt at the stables sprang to life again, more intensely this time, stabbing her with a fierceness that took her by surprise. Kaitlin had heard other girls talking of sexual feelings, but she had never quite understood what they meant. She understood now.

'Just riding,' she said saucily, over the rapid beating of her heart.

'You're a wild one, aren't you?'

'Am I?'

His eyes were on her face, lingering deliberately on her lips before going to her throat, and then to her breasts. Nobody before Flynn had ever looked at Kaitlin in quite that very male way. Oh, but he was flirtatious and blatant: he must be used to having girls falling all over him.

'The guys were right about you,' he said at last.

She danced him a flirtatious look of her own. 'Were they?'

'Sure they were. Why didn't you wait for me, Kaitlin?'

It was the first time he had used her name, the sound of it on his lips made her feel a little weak. 'I just didn't.'

'That isn't an answer, Kaitlin.'

'Best answer you're going to get, cowboy.'

In a moment, and without any warning, Flynn brought his horse up close to hers. Before Kaitlin could stop him, he had seized her reins.

'Let go,' she ordered.

'When you've answered me.'

'I don't think you heard me, Flynn.'

'I heard you very well, Kaitlin. Why didn't you wait?'

Her eyes were on the hand that held her reins. A big hand, tanned and lean and long-fingered. Kaitlin longed to touch it. Her own hand was moving towards it, when she realized what she was doing, and stopped.

Looking up, she saw his eyes gleam. *Did he know how close she'd come to touching him?*

'Why?' he asked.

'I don't have to answer you, Flynn.'

'Because you're the boss's daughter?' he drawled.

'I didn't say that,' Kaitlin countered hotly. 'I didn't even think it.'

'Glad to hear it.'

'Whatever faults I may have, I am *not* a snob.'

'That's great,' Flynn said, 'because I really do want to get to know you better.'

Still holding her reins, he leaned closer towards her. He was so close that she could feel the warmth of his breath against her face and the male smell of him in her nostrils. Tensely, Kaitlin waited.

Incredibly, Flynn drew back.

'Why?' she asked, a little unsteadily.

'Why what?' His eyes were on her lips.

'You were about to kiss me.'

'Maybe.'

'Scared?'

'Scared?' As he rocked backwards on his horse, she saw his eyes sparkling with laughter. 'I've never yet been scared of kissing a girl.'

'Kissed many?' she asked lightly.

'Dozens.'

'Anyway—' she brought a note of challenge into her voice '—I still say you're scared now.'

The big hand on her reins tightened. 'You're a tease, Kaitlin Mullins. Is that how you get your thrills—by teasing guys?'

'Don't change the subject, Flynn. We were talking about you. Are you scared?'

'No.'

'Something's holding you back though.'

'One small fact.'

She understood him immediately. 'It's what you said before, I'm the boss's daughter. That's it, isn't it? So what? Does it make me less desirable?'

'You're the most desirable female I've seen in a long time.'

'But there's my father,' Kaitlin said, hiding her pleasure.

'I wonder what he'd say if he knew I'd kissed you. And in case you want to make anything of that—I don't fancy losing my job.'

'Your job,' she said slowly.

'Know what that is, Kaitlin Mullins? Or is it something you know nothing about?'

'Of course I know, even though I haven't had a job myself, not yet. I've been at school until now.'

'Let me tell you what a job is, Kaitlin. It means security. Being able pay my own way. Having some money to send my old man every month, so that he can afford the occasional luxury.'

These were words the like of which Kaitlin had never heard, and she was ashamed. 'I'm sorry,' she said quietly.

Flynn grinned. 'Kaitlin Mullins sorry?'

'Believe it or not.'

'I do believe it,' he said unexpectedly.

'As for kissing me—' her eyes met his in a challenge '—all I see is a few cows in the distance, and I guess they won't talk.'

Flynn laughed. 'You really are wild, aren't you?'

'Am I?'

'And so sexy that I can't possibly resist you. Which is why I've been planning to kiss you since the moment I set eyes on you in the corral—father or no father.'

He was still holding her reins with one hand. The other went around her shoulders, drawing her to him. The two horses were so close now that Kaitlin's thigh was pressed against Flynn's. The warmth of his skin travelled from his arm through her blouse to her arm and neck and breast. The muscles of his thigh were hard, giving rise to sensations she had never even dreamed of.

As his lips fastened on hers, her throat was so dry that she could barely swallow. At first there was just the pressure of his lips. Then she felt his tongue, touching the outer corners of her mouth, inserting its tip between her lips; burning her, sending wild excitement coursing through every part of her body.

The kiss seemed to last forever.

When Flynn lifted his mouth, Kaitlin looked at him dazed. It was a few seconds before she could focus properly, and then she saw that his expression had changed, as well.

Flynn was the first to speak. 'It was worth it,' he said softly.

'Worth what?'

'Losing my job.'

'You won't lose your job. Nobody will ever know.'

His hand left her shoulders and went to her face, his thumb pushing a strand of damp hair from her forehead, then tracing the shape of her mouth where they had just kissed.

'It would have been worth it anyway,' Flynn said.

Kaitlin fell in love with him at that moment.

The cattle thieves were not seen again at the ranch: to all intents and purposes the threat they had posed had gone, but Kaitlin and Flynn continued to ride together.

Kaitlin's parents were surprised but pleased that their headstrong daughter was prepared to relinquish her independence, that she was willing to be accompanied when she went out on the range. A few of the cowboys commented on the fact that Flynn was often missing from the round-ups, that he did not spend as much time roping and branding and working as the others. But they knew that Flynn was only following the boss's orders, and if the hours he spent in pretty Kaitlin's company were more than just duty—well, so what? Flynn was popular with the men, and their teasing was good-natured.

There was magic in the days that followed their first meeting. Together they roamed the range, racing through the cool of an early dawn, or walking their horses slowly alongside each other when the burning heat drained even the sturdiest animals of energy. Sometimes they jumped fences or ditches, Kaitlin laughing in delight when Flynn expressed his surprise at the excellence of her riding skills.

Not a day passed without kissing. It was becoming more and more difficult for them to keep their hands and lips off each other. Alone in the grasslands, with only the birds and the horses and the grazing cattle for company, they were able to kiss and cuddle and talk, to dream of a romantic future, to make promises that their feelings would last forever.

Not that Flynn ever actually spoke the word 'love'. But Kaitlin instinctively knew that he loved her, and that his feelings for her were as strong as hers were for him. It never occurred to her that it could not be so.

'This isn't enough,' he said once, lifting his head so that they could both draw breath.

'What more do you want?' She was dazed, her lips felt bruised.

'Don't you know, sweet?'

She adored it when he used endearments. 'I guess I do.'

'All those men you've known...'

'There haven't been many, Flynn. Mainly the guys from neighbouring ranches: distances being what they are in Texas, I don't see any of them often.'

'And the men you went around with in Florida.'

'We had fun, nothing more.'

'*I* want more, Kaitlin.'

'Oh, God, Flynn...'

'You want it, too, sweet, I know you do.'

She did, he was right about that. She was young, just eighteen, and in love, her body craving fulfillment, yearning for it. It seemed to her that she could never get enough of Flynn. And yet something stopped her from going further than kissing. If only Flynn would say that he loved her, then it would all be so different.

'When, Kaitlin? When will you let me make love to you?'

'I don't know...'

'We both want it,' he insisted.

He was drawing her to him, six and a half feet of warm-blooded male. Her own body was a mass of clamouring sensation. The time would come, soon, when she would no longer be able to hold out.

His hands moved over her back, shaping themselves to her waist, and then lower, over her hips. 'Soon, sweet?' he coaxed.

She wanted him desperately. If he were to put her down

Somehow she made herself step away from those magic hands: if Flynn could be practical, she could be, too. He followed her to the bathroom.

She stood quite still as he pushed up her blouse and once more examined her back.

'Not quite as bad as I first thought,' he observed after a moment. 'Bit of soap and water, and you'll be OK in two shakes of a cat's tail.'

'Yes…'

'Why don't you get into the tub, Kaitlin?'

When they had let some water into the bath, she did as he suggested. Flynn began to clean her back, soaping and rinsing and succeeding in getting them both thoroughly wet.

At last he said, 'Those things you're wearing will have to come off.'

Despite all the time they had spent together, Kaitlin was suddenly shy. Her fingers shook as they went to the buttons of her blouse. She hadn't got further than the first button when Flynn's fingers covered hers. 'Let me do that,' he said gruffly.

She was trembling as he removed her blouse. The big hands went to her shoulders, and then to her breasts, cupping them as they had cupped her face minutes earlier, his palms hard and a little rough, unnervingly sexy as they moved slowly over her soft bare skin.

She jerked when he touched the top of her jeans. 'Is this really necessary?'

'They're getting very wet.'

When the jeans were off, Flynn ran his hands over her stomach and her hips, down over her thighs. Wherever he touched her, little fires were ignited: in no time Kaitlin's whole body was on fire.

'We're forgetting my back,' she whispered, when excitement threatened to overwhelm her.

'Right… Kneel down, Kaitlin.'

Turning her back to Flynn, she knelt, and Flynn began to attend to her scratches. After the gentleness he had displayed earlier, it came as no surprise to Kaitlin that he was gentle now too. There were more scratches than she had realized. Flynn began to work on them, patiently, one at a time.

Gentle though he was, Flynn was no nurse, and he had never done anything like this before. The bathroom floor was beginning to resemble a pool of water. Flynn was getting wet, too.

'Only one thing for it,' he announced. 'I'm getting in with you.'

In seconds he had stripped, and was in the bath, too. When the scratches on Kaitlin's back were clean, they began to splash each other. They laughed and played, getting more excited all the time as they anticipated the kissing and caressing that awaited them in Kaitlin's bedroom.

At almost the same moment the playfulness suddenly ceased. They looked at each other, dark eyes holding green ones, drinking in each other's faces as intensely as if they had never seen each other before, as if they were learning every detail of the other's face. Flynn's hands were on Kaitlin's hips, her hands lay flat-palmed on his chest. Time seemed to stand still: there was only the intensity of their eyes, and the excitement that gripped them both.

Kaitlin was the first to speak. 'Flynn...' She was trembling.

'You are so beautiful,' Flynn groaned.

'Am I?' She had never been shy with him, but there was an expression in his eyes that made her shy now.

'Beautiful. Exciting. Incredibly sexy.'

All the things she yearned to be for him. The things he was for her.

'Sure we need to wait till after your party to make love?'

Had she really made that condition? Absurd to think of it now, when every inch of her body was crying out for him. Yet something—the thought of an engagement—made her say, 'Yes.'

He made a hissing note in his throat. 'Oh, God, Kaitlin. Have you any idea how much I want you?'

She felt him throbbing against her, hard and vital, and was awed at the thought that she had the power to affect him so deeply. At the same time, her own desire was growing by the second.

'Flynn…' She stopped, not knowing what to say.

'You want it, too,' he said unsteadily.

'Only ten more days,' she managed to say.

'Ten whole days. How can we last that long?'

She was wondering the same thing. 'Maybe we shouldn't have gotten in the bath together, maybe it was a mistake,' she whispered.

'No!' he exclaimed. 'How can it be a mistake? We want each other. You want me as much as I want you, Kaitlin.'

'Flynn…'

Kaitlin opened her mouth, about to explain to Flynn why she wanted to wait, but he had reached for her again, and his lips covering hers made it impossible to speak. He was kissing her passionately now, so passionately that Kaitlin felt herself drifting to the edges of sanity.

She was startled when his head jerked back suddenly. 'What…?' She looked at him through dazed eyes.

'That sound.'

'I didn't hear anything.'

'There it is again. A car.'

This time Kaitlin heard it, too. '*My parents*! The family honk! They always sound the horn when they come home.'

'You said they'd be gone all day.' Flynn's voice reflected his shock.

'They must have changed their minds.'

'Better not let them find me here.' In a second he was out of the bath.

'We're not doing anything wrong,' Kaitlin protested.

'Try telling them so.'

'It's not as if…as if we're not committed to each other.'

'We're not engaged, Kaitlin.' Flynn was talking rapidly as he pulled on his clothes.

'We could be! Flynn…'

Let's get engaged now, she wanted to say, forgetting that she had been waiting for him to propose to her.

'This is no time to talk, Kaitlin,' he said roughly.

He didn't waste any time putting on his shoes: his feet were still wet as he hurried out of the bathroom. Kaitlin heard the front door of the house open as the back door slammed shut.

She was towelling herself dry when her mother walked into the bathroom, her eyes narrowing at the sight of the wet floor. 'All this water—what's been happening here, Kaitlin?' she demanded.

'I've been in the tub.'

'At this time of the day?'

'I fell and scratched myself, I needed a wash.'

'I see.'

Kaitlin's heart sank at the grim expression in her mother's face. 'Did you and Dad have a good time in town?' she asked, as lightly as she could. 'You're back so early.'

'Yes, we're early.' And then, 'Anything you want to tell me, Kaitlin?'

Kaitlin hesitated. She loved her mother, and she wondered whether she owed it to her to tell her what she and Flynn had been up to. No, she decided after a moment; she was eighteen, an adult. Besides, she was in love with Flynn, and words would only spoil what had happened. Very soon now, she and Flynn would announce their engagement to the world, and then their relationship would be official.

'No,' she said.

'Sure?'

'Yes.'

Half an hour later, dressed in fresh clothes, Kaitlin was about to go to the stables when her mother called her. There were party lists to go over, she said; arrangements to make. Eager to find Flynn, to talk to him after their hasty parting, Kaitlin wanted to protest. The firmness in her mother's tone stopped her. She would see Flynn tomorrow, there was no rush to talk today.

But in the stables the next day, Kaitlin stopped short at the sight of the cowboy who was busy with the horses.

'Brett,' she said in surprise. And then, 'Where's Flynn?'

'Cattle drive.' Flynn's replacement was a man of few words.

Kaitlin looked at him in disbelief. '*Cattle drive*? Flynn has gone on a cattle drive?'

'Right.'

'I don't believe it! He'd have told me.'

'Saw him leave.'

'He'd have told me,' Kaitlin said again. 'Was this something sudden or had the drive been planned?'

'Planned. Always are.'

It was true: a cattle drive, especially when big herds and large distances were involved, was seldom undertaken impulsively or without extensive arrangements. *Why hadn't Flynn told her about it*?

'Did Flynn know he was going?' she asked.

The cowboy hesitated. 'Couldn't say, miss,' he said then, his tone odd.

'Did he take someone's place?'

'Could be he did.'

That was it, Kaitlin realized, a sick feeling forming in the pit of her stomach. Flynn had deliberately chosen to absent himself from the ranch at this particular time, and there could be only one reason for it: she had disappointed him. She had played too hard to get. He had wanted to make love to her, she had known how much he wanted it, and she had refused him. True, her parents had come home just at the worst time, but Flynn knew that even if they had stayed away, Kaitlin would not have allowed him into her bed. After the party, she'd told him. What difference did a few days make, he had asked. She realized now that he'd thought she was a tease.

'When will they be back, Brett?'

'Ten days.'

Hope flared inside her. 'Which day?'

'Saturday.'

Saturday. There was still hope.

The next days were hectic, every hour filled with activity. Kaitlin, who had thought all the preparations for her party were under control, was amazed to find how much there was to take up her time.

Each morning she would look longingly out of the window in the direction of the stables, wishing that instead of yet another shopping expedition she could be in the saddle, with the wind in her hair and Star's back beneath her thighs. Longing, more than anything else, to be with Flynn; wondering what he was doing, missing him more than she would ever have believed possible.

'You're up early,' said her father, when she came into the kitchen early on Saturday morning.

'Guess I am.'

'Can't wait till tonight, honey? Excited about wearing that new party dress?'

She was excited, not about the dress but at the thought of seeing Flynn. She couldn't wait to talk to him, to touch and kiss him. She couldn't wait to tell him that contrary to anything he might have thought about her, she had never meant to be a hold-out and a tease.

As soon as she could, she made her way to the cook-house, where a few of the cowboys, those who had not gone on the cattledrive, were finishing their meal. No, they told her, the cowboys were not back yet.

She went again and again, only to be disappointed every time. The cowboys would return before evening, she told herself: they had to be back.

Half an hour before the party, she went outside again. Her dress was laid out on her bed: she should be getting dressed.

Nobody saw her as she left the house and walked to the bunkhouse where she learned that the cowboys had got back from the cattledrive.

'Where is Flynn?' she asked the nearest man.

'In the shower.'

It was getting late, she couldn't wait for him to come out.

For a moment she considered leaving a message of re-minder, but she felt embarrassed at the thought that she hadn't invited the other cowboys to the party. Next time everyone would be included, she resolved.

In any event, a reminder was unnecessary. Flynn was back at the ranch. He knew about the party, not a day had passed since the invitations had gone out that they hadn't discussed it together. Flynn knew Kaitlin was expecting him.

Where was Flynn? Again and again, Kaitlin asked herself the question.

People were arriving, some by car, many by plane. They thronged the house, the patio and the flood-lit area around the pool. So many people. The sons and daughters of ranchers. Some of the rising young men from the oilfields. Boys she had gone to school with. Some of the friends she had made in Florida.

It was a wonderful night. The sky was clear and alive with a myriad stars, and the aroma of flowers, specially ordered for the occasion, filled the air. Music played, and there was dancing.

Kaitlin, lovely in her new dress, flitted from one person to another, talking to this one, laughing with that one, dancing. And all the time part of her was watching out for Flynn.

Time passed and she began to wonder what was keeping him away? How long could it take a person to shower and dress? Could she have missed him in the crowd? But no, he was so much taller than any other man here, so much more dynamic. If Flynn was at the party, she would see him.

On the patio she asked her mother, 'Have you seen Flynn?'

'Flynn? Oh, you mean the cowboy?'

'Yes, of course!'

'He's not at the party, Katie.'

'He said he'd come, he knows I was expecting him.'

Her mother hesitated before saying, 'Do you think he'd fit in with this crowd, Katie?'

'What a question, Mom, of course, he'll fit in! He'll be the most dynamic guy in the place. The girls will all be crazy about him, the guys envious—not one of them can compare with Flynn.'

'Katie—'

'I can't imagine what in the world can be keeping him. I know he's back from the cattle drive, he should have been here by now.'

Kaitlin was the most popular girl at the party. The young men vied for her attention. She danced and danced, going from one man's arms to another. And all the time she was waiting for Flynn to arrive.

As the evening wore on, her mood changed from expectation to disappointment, and eventually to despair. Whenever she'd thought of the party, she had hoped for so much. She had dreamed of dancing with Flynn, of seeing the admiration in the eyes of her friends when she introduced them to the man she loved. She had even—and this was the very pinnacle of her dreams—imagined an engagement.

Where was Flynn? Why had he stayed away from the party?

Ten o'clock came and went. At eleven, she decided she wouldn't wait any longer. When a dance ended, Kaitlin vanished into the shadows at the edge of the patio. Nobody stopped her as she ran down the steps and away from the house.

Quickly she walked down the path that led to the bunkhouse. Through the open windows she heard talking and the sound of a guitar.

The talking stopped abruptly when she opened the door, and after a moment the guitar-player ended his strumming. The cowboys stared at her in amazement.

She looked back at them. 'Where is Flynn?'

Nobody answered, but some of the men exchanged uneasy glances.

At the back of Kaitlin's neck the small hairs prickled. 'Please. Where is Flynn?'

The silence continued. Kaitlin was beginning to feel a little ill. 'I have to know. Please. Please, tell me.'

'In town,' Brett said.

'*In town*! He's supposed to be at my party. I don't understand.' Kaitlin took a step towards Brett. 'Do you know where to find him?' And when the cowboy nodded, 'If I get a car, will you take me to him?'

Again the exchange of glances. In the bunkhouse the tension was mounting.

A minute passed. Then Brett said, 'Prefer not to.'

'*Please*! It's important to me.'

This time, unwillingly, reluctantly, the cowboy agreed.

They found Flynn in a bar. On a Formica table in front of him was a tankard of beer and two glasses. Beside him, very close to him, was a red-headed woman with heavily mascaraed eyes.

Kaitlin's legs turned weak in an instant. 'My God,' she whispered in shock.

Flynn had not seen her. Putting his hand on her arm, Brett tried to draw her out of the bar. 'Come…'

For a moment Kaitlin was tempted to go with him. Leave Flynn alone with his bimbo. Retreat before he saw her. Hold on to her pride, her dignity. She could deal with the situation next day, at the ranch, alone with Flynn.

She took a step backwards, then stopped. *She* had nothing to be ashamed of. Giving herself no time for second thoughts, she strode up to the table. 'Flynn!'

He looked up. Just for a second, an expression crossed his face. Regret? Embarrassment? But the expression, whatever it was, quickly vanished.

'Hi, Kaitlin.'

'What are you doing here?'

'Having a good time.' He drew the woman onto his lap and she cuddled against him. 'This is my friend. Her name's Marietta.'

Kaitlin ignored the introduction. Over the horribly sick feeling in her throat and her mouth, she said, very calmly, 'You were coming to my party.'

'Oh, the party. Right.'

'I waited for you.'

'Did you?'

'Why didn't you come?'

He shrugged. 'Does it matter?'

The sickness intensified. The taste on her tongue was vile. 'What are you doing here?'

'Told you—having a good time. A good time with a woman. A *real* woman, Kaitlin. One who doesn't play games. Who knows how to give a man what he wants.'

Was this how it was all going to end? The excitement, the joy, the all-consuming love. Was it all ending here, in this sleazy place, with some bimbo sneering up at her, and the man she loved hurting her with every contemptuous word he spoke?

To Kaitlin's horror, Flynn bent his head and pressed a kiss against Marietta's lips.

Tersely, determined that she would not give way to tears, Kaitlin said, 'I don't want to see you again, Flynn.'

'You won't have to. I'm leaving the ranch.'

'Leaving?' Her lips were trembling.

'Tomorrow morning.'

Kaitlin spun around, away from the table. She was walking quickly towards the door, Brett at her side, when Flynn called her name.

'Kaitlin.'

She turned her head. 'Yes?'

'I'll be back. Five years from today.'

'I won't be around to welcome you.'

'I'll be back, Kaitlin. And when I come, I'll take over the ranch.'

'Like hell you will! Dad will see you horse-whipped first.'

'Five years from today, Kaitlin. Believe it.'

'In your dreams, Flynn.'

He was talking absolute nonsense, of course. The meaningless words of someone who'd had too much to drink. The ranch would never belong to Flynn Henderson.

But there was a certain tone in his voice, a strange ring of conviction, as if he meant what he said.

CHAPTER FIVE

THIS time, when Flynn landed the plane at the ranch, Kaitlin did not look at all surprised to see him.

'I figured you'd be back,' she said evenly.

Dark eyes gleamed. 'You could at least pretend to be happy to see me.'

A challenging gaze met his. '*Happy*? Are you kidding? Why on earth would I be happy when I know you're only here to make my life more difficult than it already is?'

As Flynn looked down at her, it came to him that *he* was extraordinarily happy to see *her*. She looked as if she'd stepped out of the pool minutes earlier, and, for once, she showed no signs of fatigue. In fact, she was looking quite lovely in a blouse that was almost exactly the same shade as her eyes, and jeans that clung snugly to long shapely legs. Lovely and extremely sexy.

For five years Flynn had carried inside him a deep anger towards Kaitlin Mullins. Yet the more he saw of her now, the more difficult it was becoming to hold on to that anger.

'That is why you're here, isn't it?' she was saying.

'To make your life difficult? Depends how you look at things.'

'Have you come to collect payment?'

'Partly.'

'Partly…? Flynn, we need to talk.'

'Oh?'

'About my payments.'

Beneath the crisp tone, Flynn sensed a hint of despair, and wished he did not feel such a deep longing to protect and cherish her. Compassion for Kaitlin had never been a part of his plan. How then had the emotion become such an integral part of his psyche?

'I have to tell you—' she began.

'Later,' he interrupted. 'We'll talk about your payments later, after we've gone riding.'

'*Riding*?'

'You seem surprised.'

'If I am, it's because I don't believe for a moment you came out all this way for a ride. You can find a horse anywhere, Flynn, any time you want.'

There it was again, the autocratic Mullins manner. Like parents like daughter, that was the thought he must hold on to.

Coolly, Flynn said, 'I want to ride the range. *This* range.'

Kaitlin's expression changed. 'You want to look around your investment.'

'Don't you think that makes good business sense?'

'I'd have thought a person would want to see an investment *before* granting a mortgage,' she said tersely. 'Of course, in your case it's different—you already know the ranch like the back of your hand.'

'I'm sure I can still find my way around blindfold,' he agreed. 'But there's more to it than geography. Last time I was here I noticed how the *mesquite* had spread. I need to see the stock and the state of your pasture land.'

Green eyes flashed. 'Bit late for all that, isn't it? Bill Seally won't go back on the deal at this stage.'

He let the retort pass. 'Let's get the horses, Kaitlin.'

'One horse, Flynn. If you want to ride, you can ride by yourself.'

'I want you to come with me.'

Kaitlin stared at him a long moment, her eyes sparkling with rebellion. But when Flynn went to the stables she went with him: perhaps, he thought, because she understood there was no point in useless battle when she still had other battles left to fight.

The tension that lay between them lessened by the time they reached the grasslands. Here at last they were able to give rein to the horses, letting them gallop at will. Flynn, who no longer rode as often as he used to, experienced the special elation that filled him whenever he was on a horse.

Kaitlin passed him, a slip of a girl, totally at home in the saddle. When she turned her head, he saw that her eyes

were sparkling. Above the clop of the horses' hooves, rang
the clear bell-like sound of her laughter.

This was how it had been five years ago, Flynn and
Kaitlin, riding the range together. Almost, *almost*, Flynn
was able to believe that the parting had never occurred. The
thought that came into his mind was involuntary: *can things
be different this time?*

And then he remembered Kaitlin's sharp reaction to the
idea of marriage, and he told himself not to be a damn fool.

Deliberately, he turned his attention to his surroundings.
An outsider might have been favourably impressed with the
ranch. But Flynn observed the signs that suggested lack of
money, shortage of labour, and a general air of sloppiness
which had not been present here five years earlier.

'Still haven't seen any cowboys,' he told Kaitlin when
he rode up beside her.

'You will,' she informed him, and led the way to a section where cattle were being branded.

Flynn was all cowboy now, his eyes taking in every detail. The noise and the dust, the cowboys darting in and out
of the herd, roping the cattle before branding them with the
distinctive mark of the ranch.

It was a while before the men noticed Kaitlin and Flynn.
A few had been at the ranch a long time, and when they
took a break from their work they crowded around Flynn.

'Flynn! Great to see you!'

'Where've you been, man?'

'Say, Flynn, heard you were bull-riding on the circuit.
Make lots of money?'

'Bull-riding, and still in one piece! However did you
manage it?'

'Can you still rope a steer?' one of the men laughingly
challenged.

'Watch me,' came the easy answer.

Taking a lariat from one of the cowboys, Flynn rode his
horse into the herd. In no time he had selected a steer, roped
it and taken it to be branded.

'Great roping,' observed one of the older cowboys. 'You
must have made a pile of money in rodeo.'

Flynn grinned, then began to engage the men in ranch

talk. His questions were direct and to the point, and the men answered him readily.

'Coming back to the ranch?' asked Brett.

'One day perhaps,' he said lightly, and the cowboys were content to leave it at that.

They rode further. When they were alongside each other, Kaitlin said, 'The guys were right, that was great roping, cowboy.'

He grinned at her. 'Thanks.'

'Thirty seconds flat.'

'You were counting?'

'Every second.'

'Do you always do that?'

'No.'

'Why this time?'

'Thought I'd see if you could beat the time you took to rope my lost calf.'

'Did I?'

'You were close. You don't need anyone to tell you that not another man on this ranch comes anywhere near you for speed.'

Flynn studied her, five and a half feet of angry, challenging female. 'Where's all this leading to, Kaitlin? Because I know it's leading somewhere.'

'You showed off with the rope, Flynn.'

'I was asked to do it,' he reminded her.

'So you were. But you were showing off all the same. Flynn Henderson, grand star of the rodeo circuit.'

He looked at her inquiringly. 'So, Kaitlin?'

'Not a word to the cowboys about the mortgage. Not a single word about your real reason for being at the ranch.'

'Do you think it concerns them at this moment?'

'Brett asked if you were thinking of coming back to the ranch.'

'And I told him maybe I would.'

'He thought you were coming back as a cowboy.'

'I know what he thought.'

'I don't suppose you considered telling him the truth.'

'Of course not. And to answer your next question—because I know it's right there on the end of that rosy-tipped tongue—I didn't think the time was right.'

'It's not going to happen, Flynn.'

'Isn't it, Kaitlin?'

'No! Despite your famous promise. I won't let it happen.'

Flynn looked down into a small oval face that was all challenge and defiance. 'Just as well I didn't say anything to Brett in that case.'

'I just want you to know that I'll die before letting you take over this ranch.'

He grinned at her. 'Let's hope it doesn't come to that, Kaitlin.'

Flynn was in the lead when they came to a point where the trail they were on intersected with another. Instead of continuing toward the stables, Flynn took the new trail instead.

'Wrong way,' Kaitlin told him.

'Right way,' he said.

'Where are you going, Flynn? There's nothing to see here.' Her voice was tense.

His expression, as he turned to look at her, was enigmatic. 'Isn't there?'

'No. Except...' She stopped.

'The cabin.' He took in the sudden flush staining her cheeks, the storminess in her eyes. 'Go there often, Kaitlin?'

'Haven't been there in years,' she said shortly.

'All the more reason to go there now.'

'I don't want to go to the cabin, Flynn.'

'I do.'

'Go alone, in that case. I'll see you back at the ranch-house.'

She was about to turn her horse, when he leaned towards her. 'Come with me, Kaitlin.'

Not for the first time their eyes met, clashed, held. Kaitlin was the first to look away. 'No,' she whispered at last.

'Humour me.'

'There's no going back, Flynn. The past is over. Don't you understand?' Her voice was unsteady.

'Perhaps I'm thinking of the future.'

'There's no future for us, Flynn. There can't be.'

Oh, but she was so quick with her answers. Only now he was no longer the callow young man he had been five years earlier. He did not run away from rejection. And he did hold some trump cards.

'I want to see the cabin,' he insisted quietly. 'Come with me, Kaitlin.'

'Flynn—'

'Please,' he said.

He directed his horse in the direction of the cabin. After a few seconds, Kaitlin followed him on her horse.

A few minutes of riding brought them to the place that even now appeared to Flynn sometimes in his dreams. Had he not known exactly where to find it, he might have missed it, for the cabin was surrounded by trees, and the short path leading away from the trail was covered with undergrowth.

Reining in his horse, Flynn looked at Kaitlin. 'Does nobody ever come here?'

'Not that I know of.' Her tone was brittle.

Flynn's gaze swept her tense face. Softly he said, 'Our own special place, Kaitlin.'

'Long ago.'

'Long ago,' he agreed.

Jumping off his horse, he looked up at Kaitlin. 'You will come in with me, won't you?'

'I really don't want to.' Her lips were stiff, her cheeks pale.

'I'm asking you to,' he said quietly.

'What's the point, Flynn?' Her voice shook.

'There doesn't have to be a point to everything, Kaitlin—don't you know that?'

'Then why are we here?'

'To look.'

'To remember?'

'That, too.'

'Remembering can be dangerous.'

'Not necessarily. It's not dangerous when—' he paused, before going on deliberately '—when the things remembered were not very meaningful in the first place.'

'You're saying that what happened here meant nothing to you?' The brittle quality in her voice was more pronounced.

It had meant everything in the world to him, at least for a while. In this cabin amid the pines Flynn had learned about tenderness and softness and femininity. For a while he had thought he'd found love. It was only afterwards that he had been confronted with humiliation and betrayal.

'We had fun here.' He made his voice deliberately cool.

'That's what it was to you, Flynn? Fun?' Kaitlin flung the words at him.

'Was it anything else to you, Kaitlin?'

Her face was turned away from him, as if Kaitlin had suddenly noticed something important in the pines to one side of the cabin.

'Was it anything other than fun?' Flynn persisted.

'It's all so long ago,' she said, still without looking at him. 'So much has happened since then.'

'You haven't answered the question.'

This time she did look at him. 'I thought I had.'

'No.' He kept all emotion out of his voice.

Kaitlin shrugged. 'I think you're making too much of this. A boy and a girl. Doing the things boys and girls do when they're alone together. Isn't that what it was all about, Flynn?' Her head swung up, and now her eyes held his. 'Was there more, Flynn? Or have I answered the question?'

Damn Kaitlin Mullins. Putting him in his place as her mother had once done. She did not have to say more. The men Kaitlin had known five years ago—the sons of wealthy ranchers, the college boys she'd romped with in Florida—all of them had lived far away. But Flynn, the cowboy, had always been around, always available for a good time.

He gave a short hard laugh. 'You've answered the question, Kaitlin.'

'Good. Then we can ride on.'

'When we've seen the cabin.'

'I'll wait for you here.'

'We'll see it together, Kaitlin.'

Giving her no chance to protest or to ride off without him, he reached up, clasped her waist in his hands, and drew her from her horse.

'Macho man,' Kaitlin hissed, and Flynn laughed.

When he had tethered both horses, he took Kaitlin's hand. Strangely, she did not resist him. Because the past reached out to her as it reached to him?

He had forgotten the feel of her hand in his: small, warm, dainty. He wove his fingers through hers: when he stroked her thumb in the way she used to like, the movement was instinctive, made without thinking.

Hand in hand they walked to the cabin, as they had walked there years earlier. Only then they had moved quickly, eager to get inside the shelter where they could kiss and caress away from prying eyes. Now they walked slowly. Kaitlin, Flynn noticed, was dragging her feet.

Outside the cabin they paused. The walls were pitted, the roof was badly in need of repair: it looked as if nobody had been here for years.

The door of the cabin was unlocked. Flynn pushed it open. Kaitlin pulled her hand out of his as they went inside.

The air was musty. A startled mouse scampered across the floor and out of sight. Dust was thick on the floor and on the few pieces of furniture.

'Strange,' Flynn mused.

'What is?' Kaitlin asked in a whisper, almost as if ghosts from the past would overhear them if they spoke loudly.

'Apart from the dust and neglect, nothing's changed. It's as if the place was waiting for us to come back here.'

'What nonsense.' But Kaitlin's tone lacked conviction.

'Is it nonsense?' Flynn asked, turning to her.

His arms were around her before she could draw breath to protest. She was so much smaller than he was, that he lifted her from the ground so that their faces would be at the same level, and so light that he felt as if he was holding a doll. Yet fragile though she was, Kaitlin was all woman. A warm-skinned woman, with sweetly-smelling hair brushing against his face, breasts that strained against him, and a rapid heartbeat that he could feel through his clothes and hers. A woman who, despite her constant show of feisty independence, was so overwhelmingly delicate and feminine that she made him feel big and male.

'Flynn?' Kaitlin said softly.

He didn't want to hear what she had to say. If she had a question, he was in no mood to answer it. There was only one thing he wanted to do just then.

Drawing her even closer, he began to kiss her. Her lips were soft and warm and trembling against his, lips that a man could kiss forever and never grow tired of kissing. Flynn let his mouth relearn the shape and feel of Kaitlin's face, the curve of her cheeks, the shape of her eyebrows, the pert nose, the eyelashes that flickered like feathers in a breeze. Back to her lips then, touching them with his tongue now, coaxing them apart. At first Kaitlin resisted, but Flynn kept up the pressure of his tongue. Just when he thought she would never give in, he heard a hissing sigh, and then her lips were opening to his. Her mouth was just as sweet-tasting as he remembered, he felt he could never get enough of it. Somewhere on the periphery of his mind he was aware of her arms lifting, hesitating, touching his arms; and then, suddenly, her hands had curved around his neck.

His whole body was on fire now, he throbbed with the longing to make love to her. Putting her down on the ground, he said, 'Wait.'

Tearing off his shirt, he spread it over the bed. Then he turned back to Kaitlin. To his dismay, he saw that she was moving towards the door.

'What are you doing?' he asked.

'What are *you* doing, Flynn?'

'The bed's dusty, we'll lie on the shirt.'

'We won't lie anywhere. Not together.'

It came to him that her tone had changed. There was a hardness in it now that was at odds with the soft hesitancy he had heard when they had first entered the cabin.

'What are you saying, Kaitlin?'

'I don't have to spell it out for you, Flynn.'

'Try.'

'Do you really think I'll lie on that bed with you?'

'If you don't think my shirt is adequate, we can go to your room at the ranch-house.'

Her lips trembled a little, but there was nothing undecided about her words. 'Don't you understand, Flynn? I have no intention of lying with you anywhere.'

'Why not?' he demanded.

'If you really want to know, I don't go in for one-night stands.'

'Is that how you see this?' he demanded.

Her shrug looked a little forced. 'What else can it possibly be?'

'A one-night stand—despite the past?'

'Such as it was.' Kaitlin's tone was hard.

'Such as it was?' he repeated, his voice hard, too, now.

'If you're honest, Flynn, you know it wasn't much. If it had been—' She stopped.

'You were saying?' he asked after a moment.

'It doesn't matter.'

'You were saying something.'

'Nothing of consequence. As I keep telling you, the past is over. We... We were very young, Flynn, and we enjoyed each other's company for a while. But that's all there ever was to it.'

So that was how it had been for her. Her parents had been right after all. Fool that he was to have thought there could have been more.

'There's no point in rehashing it,' Kaitlin said. 'As for what we have now... It's nothing more than a business relationship.'

'What we had a few minutes ago was passion,' he said evenly. 'Neither of us were thinking about business.'

'Flynn...'

'You can kid yourself all you want, Kaitlin. You can tell yourself any number of things, but if you're honest you'll admit that you're lying. I felt your heart racing. And you did put your hands around my neck.'

'Don't go on with this!' she said.

But he went on relentlessly. 'You opened your mouth to me, Kaitlin. I didn't force you.'

She stared up at him, and even in the dim light of the cabin he could see that she was trembling.

'Until I stopped to take off my shirt, you weren't thinking about business, Kaitlin.'

'Maybe not.' Her chin lifted. 'I… I admit I was a little crazy, but the craziness was temporary. We shouldn't have come here, Flynn. I tried telling you that, but you wouldn't listen.'

'We used to have fun in this cabin, Kaitlin.'

At her sides, her hands clenched. 'So you said earlier. The thing is, there's no time for fun in my life any more.' For a moment she hesitated. Then she said, 'Sometimes I wonder if I still know what fun is.'

Flynn felt something wrench inside him. Softly he said, 'What we had just now was fun, Kaitlin.'

'Maybe so.' The words sounded as if they had been wrung from her by force. 'But that's all it was. We can't recapture the past, Flynn. What we had is over, it was over a long time ago. I wish Bill had never ceded the mortgage to you, but the fact is he did. And now I have to live with my obligations to you. I need to talk about payment Flynn.'

His voice hardened once more. 'Talk away.'

Kaitlin's eyes moved to the bed, then skittered away from it. 'Not in here.'

'Why not?' Flynn taunted. 'Scared that what happened once will happen again?'

'Of course not!'

'Perhaps you're scared that next time you won't be able to stop.'

'I'm not scared,' she told him firmly. 'I can take care of myself, Flynn, and when I say no, I mean it. But we do have to discuss business, and this place—' once more her eyes went to the bed '—isn't the right place for it.'

His eyes went over the woman who still had the power to stir him as no other woman had ever been able to do. His gaze lingered on sweetly-shaped lips, on a throat in whose hollow a pulse beat a fast tattoo. He could still taste her on his tongue, his arms tingled where he had held her. He longed to pull her back into his arms—but he knew better than to do so.

Could he be falling in love with her all over again? Perish the thought! He could just imagine what Kaitlin Mullins would make of *that* possibility.

'Guess you're right,' he agreed flatly. 'This isn't the place to talk.'

'Your first payment is due a week from Friday,' he told her.

They were in the family room of the ranch-house: a lovely room, all white cane furniture with green cushions, bright yet cool. Kaitlin's mother had loved gardening, and Kaitlin, it seemed, shared that passion for there were pot-plants everywhere.

'A week from Friday?' Kaitlin repeated tensely.

'Shouldn't surprise you. You'd have had to pay Bill Seally then, too.'

'Yes, but Bill…' Kaitlin stopped, catching her upper lip between small pearl-white teeth.

'Bill was lenient. Bill didn't care about dates. Bill was so easy about money that a little more or less never bothered him—or so he said.'

'Don't put him down, Flynn.'

'I'm just putting into words your rosy-hued thoughts about Bill. But perhaps you were wrong all along, Kaitlin. Perhaps Bill Seally, rich though he is, cared very much that you were taking advantage of him.'

'I never did that,' she protested hotly. 'At least, never purposely.'

'No point in debating the matter, Kaitlin. I see it one way, you see it another. Fact is, there's a payment due.' Flynn paused, then continued deliberately. 'And I intend you to make it.'

Kaitlin stared at him. Her eyes were wide and green and unhappy.

'I'll be here next week to collect it,' Flynn said.

Kaitlin's eyes held his a second longer. Then, without a word, she left her chair and went to the window. Flynn was silent as she stood with her back to him and looked over her ranch. A stranger might have thought her composed and

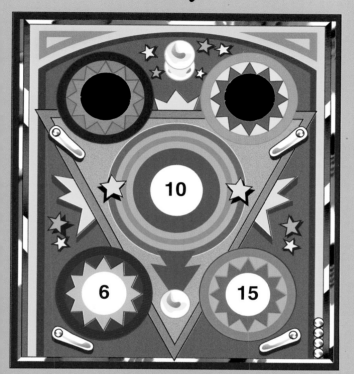

"PINBALL WIZ"

Scratch the gold circles and claim up to

4 FREE Books
and a FREE Gift!

See inside ↗

NO RISK, NO OBLIGATION TO BUY... NOW OR EVER!

How to play "PINBALL WIZ" and be eligible to receive up to FIVE FREE GIFTS!...

1. With a coin, carefully scratch away the gold circles opposite. Then, including the numbers on the front of this card, count up your total pinball score and check the conversion table to see how many FREE books and gifts you are eligible to receive.

2. Send back this card and you'll receive specially selected Mills & Boon® romances from the Enchanted™ series. These books are yours to keep absolutely FREE.

3. There's no catch. You're under no obligation to buy anything. We charge you nothing for your first shipment. And you don't have to make a minimum number of purchases - not even one!

4. The fact is, thousands of readers enjoy receiving books by mail from the Reader Service™. They like the convenience of home delivery and they like getting the best new romance novels at least a month before they are available in the shops. And of course, postage and packing is completely FREE!

5. We hope that after receiving your free books you'll want to remain a subscriber. But the choice is yours - to continue or cancel, anytime at all! So why not accept our no-risk invitation. You'll be glad you did!

A SPECIAL GIFT FOR YOU IF YOU SCORE OVER 51 POINTS!

You'll look a million dollars when you wear this lovely necklace! Its cobra-link chain is a generous 18" long, and the lustrous simulated pearl completes this attractive gift.

NOT ACTUAL SIZE

Play
"PINBALL WIZ"

▶ Up to 4 free Enchanted™ novels
▶ A free simulated pearl necklace

PINBALL WIZ POINTS CONVERSION TABLE	
Score 51 or more	**WORTH 4 FREE BOOKS** PLUS A SIMULATED PEARL NECKLACE
Score 41 to 50	**WORTH 4 FREE BOOKS**
Score 31 to 40	**WORTH 3 FREE BOOKS**
Score 30 or under	**WORTH 2 FREE BOOKS**

YES! I have scratched off the gold circles. Please send me all the gifts for which I qualify. I understand that I am under no obligation to purchase any books, as explained on the opposite page. I am over 18 years of age.

N8BI

MS/MRS/MISS/MR   INITIALS

BLOCK CAPITALS PLEASE

SURNAME

ADDRESS

POSTCODE

THE READER SERVICE™
FREEPOST SEA3794
CROYDON,
Surrey
CR9 3AQ

2

▼ DETACH AND RETURN THIS CARD TODAY, NO STAMP NEEDED! ▼

confident, but Flynn, who knew Kaitlin so well, was not fooled. He registered the slight droop of her shoulders, a quiver in the hands at her sides.

A minute passed. At length Kaitlin turned back into the room.

'I can't do it,' she said tonelessly. 'At least, not by next week.'

'Sorry to hear it.'

'Flynn... Flynn, I need time.'

'Suppose I'm not interested?'

Kaitlin was pale beneath her tan, but her shoulders straightened. A fighter to the end, Flynn thought.

'I guess you know,' he said quietly, 'what happens to people who can't meet their obligations.'

'You wouldn't foreclose?' Kaitlin was unable to keep the quiver from her voice. 'You can't do it, Flynn.'

'I can, and you know it.'

She took a step towards him, and her hand touched his arm. In a second he felt desire coursing through him.

'Flynn... We were friends once.'

'A long time ago, as you never tire of reminding me.'

The hand left his arm, as abruptly as if it had been singed by a flame. 'That's true,' she said.

Once more she turned away. Flynn waited.

After a minute Kaitlin looked back at him. 'All I'm asking for is time. I'll pay you, really I will.' The last words were spoken with a fierce intensity. 'I need an extension.'

'No,' said Flynn.

'You'd really do this to me?' The lovely eyes were stark with despair.

Flatly Flynn said, 'You're talking emotion, Kaitlin. I'm talking business.'

'I'm talking my home.' Kaitlin's voice throbbed with passion. 'My beloved home, Flynn. I was born and raised on this ranch. My grandfather bought the land, my father lived here all his life. And you'd take it all away from me, because of a plan you dreamed up five years ago.'

'That's right.'

Kaitlin's eyes were bright with tears, but she seemed to be trying very hard to keep them at bay. 'Two options—is that all I have, Flynn? Either you get paid next Friday, or you take the ranch?'

She was swallowing hard, but despite all her efforts, two tears escaped her eyes and rolled onto her cheeks. Flynn wondered if she had any idea how beautiful she was at that moment.

Pushing at the tears with her fingers, she said, 'In case you think I'm crying, Flynn, I'm not.'

He touched a damp cheek. 'Aren't you, Kaitlin?'

'No! But to get back to business—do I really have only two options?'

He was silent a moment. Then he said, 'Three, actually.'

She looked at him. 'Three…'

He was suddenly very angry. Had his offer meant so little to her that she had already forgotten it?

'We talked about it the last time I was here. I take over the ranch—and you marry me.'

Flynn found himself holding his breath as he looked down at Kaitlin. One emotion seemed to chase another in the small oval face: emotions that he wished he could read, but couldn't. Something flared, like flame, in the blue eyes, and then died just as quickly—what was it?

After a moment she said flatly, 'No, Flynn.'

'I'm offering you a way out of your troubles.'

'It's no way at all, Flynn.'

'No more worries about money. No moving out of your home. Your life wouldn't change, Kaitlin.'

'Except in one major way—I'd be married.'

He held her gaze steadily, masking his anger at yet another one of Kaitlin Mullins's rejections. 'Would that be so bad?'

'I can't bear the thought,' she said bitterly.

Something drove him to continue. 'We got on well once. We even talked about being married some day.'

'Childish talk,' she said unsteadily. 'It didn't mean anything.'

'Didn't it?'

'In the light of…' She stopped.

In the light of what?

She looked away from him. 'It doesn't matter. Not now.

We were young, unrealistic. Now....' Again she stopped, her lips quivering slightly. 'It wouldn't be right,' she said at last. 'For either of us.'

His eyes flicked over her face. 'You're not interested in marriage?'

'Not the kind you have in mind. When I get married, Flynn—*if* I get married—it will be for love. Mutual love, Flynn. Nothing less will do.'

'I see,' he said after a long pause.

'As for the ranch—' she was looking at him once more '—I won't sell it to you. I can't stop you from foreclosing, but I'll never willingly give up the ranch to you.'

'I've offered you a good price,' Flynn said grimly.

'It's a question of principles.'

'You're a fool, Kaitlin Mullins,' Flynn said flatly. 'Principles won't buy you the necessities of life, they won't keep you clothed or put food on your table.'

'That's true, but I'll never live with the shame of knowing that I betrayed my parents.'

What had her parents ever done to deserve such loyalty, Flynn wondered. His lips tightened. 'In that case, there's nothing left to say.'

'Except to ask you once more—won't you consider giving me a little time?'

'How much time?' he asked abruptly.

She took a breath. 'A month.'

'You know better than to ask me that.'

'Three weeks?'

His eyes didn't leave her face. 'How do you think you'd come up with the money?'

'I'd find a way.'

Flynn wondered whether she was trying to convince him or herself.

Quietly, he said, 'Do you really believe you can raise the money, Kaitlin?'

'I have to. I will.' There was a hint of despair in her voice.

'Don't you think you're just postponing the inevitable? That sooner or later you'll find yourself having to give up the ranch?'

'I'll never give it up,' she said passionately. 'I'll work myself to the bone if I have to. Somehow I'll find the money I need.'

'I'll say this,' Flynn told her, admiration creeping into his tone, 'your parents didn't have half your spunk and energy.'

Kaitlin's cheeks reddened angrily. 'Keep my parents out of this. Any arrangement we might have has nothing to do with them.'

As Flynn looked down at her, he wondered how it was possible for so much spirit, energy and defiance to be contained in five and a half feet of slender womanhood.

'There is one other way,' he said at last.

'What are you talking about?'

'A way that would benefit us both.'

Hope flared in her eyes. '*Tell me*!'

'You could work off the payments, Kaitlin.'

'I don't understand. What would I do, Flynn?'

'You'd render services instead of money.'

'What sort of services, Flynn?'

'Personal ones.'

'*Personal*?' In an instant, green eyes had turned stormy and the colour in her cheeks had intensified.

Flynn's own eyes sparkled. 'Why are you so upset, Kaitlin? I haven't defined the word "personal".'

'You don't have to,' she said furiously. 'How naive do you think I am? I never guessed you'd sink so low, Flynn. Though perhaps I should have known. Oh, but you're a rotten swine, Flynn Henderson. Even if I was starving, I wouldn't consider what you're proposing! The answer is no.'

Politely, Flynn asked, 'What exactly are you saying no to?'

'Want me to put it into words? Sex. S.E.X. I won't marry you, so you find another way of getting me into your bed. Whose bed were you thinking of anyway, Flynn? Yours or mine? I don't even know where your bed is. Not that it matters, because I'll never sleep in it. Just as you won't sleep in mine.'

'I haven't asked you to sleep with me, Kaitlin.'

She took a step backwards. 'Isn't that what you were getting at?'

'No.' A wicked grin. 'Though I don't deny I'd like to share a bed with you. You were always sexy, Kaitlin, and you're even sexier now. I'll bet we could enjoy each other.'

Her flush intensified. 'If you didn't mean sex, what did you mean, Flynn?'

A strand of fair hair had escaped her pony-tail. Flynn touched it, relishing the softness between his fingertips before he tucked it behind one of her ears. Kaitlin did not push him away. She stood very still, her eyes holding his, and Flynn wondered if she was as aware of him as he was of her.

Softly, he said, 'There are other personal services, Kaitlin.'

'I can't think of any.' Her voice shook.

'For one thing, you could help me choose some new clothes.'

She stared at him in amazement. 'Why would you want that?'

'I'm basically a cowboy, Kaitlin, a man with a Stetson and a comfortable pair of boots. Give me a hand-tooled leather belt, and I know what I'm looking at.'

'Then you don't need my help.'

'But I do. I've already told you I'm involved in the oil business. There's an oilmen's convention coming up. People will be there, many of them very wealthy.'

Her expression revealed comprehension. 'You don't want to attend the convention wearing cowboy clothes.'

'Exactly. That's where you come in, Kaitlin. At heart, I'll always be a cowboy. But you…you know about the kind of clothes city people wear.'

'What exactly are you asking me to do, Flynn?'

'We'll fly to Austin, and you'll go shopping with me. Will you do it, Kaitlin?'

'If I say yes—and I haven't said I will, Flynn—what would it mean for me?'

He grinned at her. 'Half of the next payment taken care of.'

'Half the payment!' She looked stunned. 'Do you mean that?'

'Wouldn't say it if I didn't. What do you say, Kaitlin?'

What was Flynn up to now? He had to be up to something, she reflected. Tempted as she was to take him up on his offer, she had to know his motives.

'Tell me more,' she said coolly.

'More?'

'You never do anything without a reason.'

'I told you my reason. I need help choosing clothes.'

'For which you're prepared to forego payment. Pretty strange, if you ask me. You must know dozens of women who could help you.'

'Dozens?' A rakish eyebrow lifted in amusement. 'I know a few. Thing is, Kaitlin, none of them have your qualifications.'

'Which are?'

'A lifetime of being spoiled and indulged,' he drawled.

Outraged, Kaitlin stared at Flynn. 'You make me sound like a poor little rich girl,' she exploded.

'Your words, Kaitlin, not mine,' he told her pleasantly. 'Fact is, shopping expeditions used to be part of your life.'

'Nowhere near as often as you're making out,' she said angrily.

'Often enough. Any time little Kaitlin wanted something, her parents would buy it for her. So, who better to help me make my own purchases?'

'You've made your point.' Kaitlin did her best to keep the hurt she felt out of her tone.

'Then you'll come?'

'I don't seem to have much choice.'

'No,' he conceded, in a tone that made her want to hit him.

'When do we go?'

'Tomorrow, if possible. Does that give you enough time to arrange with the men to look after the ranch?'

Kaitlin looked up to find Flynn grinning down at her, a devil-may-care grin that sent her pulses racing. If only, she thought, he was inviting her to go with him because he wanted her company, but that wasn't the case.

Flatly she said, 'I'll speak to the cowboys in the cook-house when they come in for their dinner.'

'Great. Tomorrow morning then,' Flynn said.

CHAPTER SIX

KAITLIN was finishing her breakfast the next morning, when she heard a plane in the sky. Running outside, she looked up and saw it circling overhead. It dipped, soared, dipped again and made two more circles. Kaitlin thought she saw Flynn wave in the moment before he flew off in the direction of the airstrip.

Poor little rich girl... Any time little Kaitlin wanted something her parents would buy it for her. The hateful words pulsed in her mind as she made her way quickly back into the house.

It would be a few minutes before Flynn arrived in her kitchen: there was something she needed to do before he came.

The phone was answered on the third ring. 'Hello?' A cheerful greeting.

'Hi, Anne. This is Kaitlin.'

'Kaitlin...' A hesitation that lasted a second too long. 'How are you?'

Kaitlin decided to ignore the sudden wariness in Anne Seally's tone. 'Good, thanks. Anne, may I speak to Bill, please?'

Kaitlin thought she heard the sound of whispering in the background. Then Ann said, 'Gee, Kaitlin, I'm sorry but he has already left.'

Kaitlin took a breath. 'When can I speak to him, Anne?'

'I... Well, I don't know... He's out now, and I can't say when he'll be back. You know how it is, honey, it's really hard to keep track of a man.'

Strange words indeed from a protective wife, who seemed always to know the whereabouts of her husband.

'I'm wondering how I can reach him, Anne. He's never there when I call.'

'I'm sorry, honey, I guess you keep missing him.'

Kaitlin's hand tightened on the receiver. 'Would you tell Bill that I called, Anne?'

'Sure I will, the moment he gets in.'

'Thanks.'

With the conversation about to end, Anne's tone took on an eagerness that was transparently phony. Anne would not make a good actress, Kaitlin thought. 'We must get together some time soon, honey. We keep talking about it, Bill and I. We've just been so busy... The children and grand-children, Bill's work... Well, you know how it is. But we'll make a plan and get together for a nice long visit.'

'Great,' Kaitlin said noncommittally, though she doubted the get-together would ever take place.

They were airborne when Flynn said, 'I want you to prom-ise me something.'

Kaitlin looked into dark eyes sparkling with mischief. 'Depends what you're asking.'

'Tell me you won't spend the day thinking of all the work you should be doing here. Promise me you'll have a good time.'

Some time during the night Kaitlin had resolved that she would not lose sight of the fact that the trip into town was nothing more than a service; that she would remain cool and reserved in all her dealings with Flynn. But that was easier said than done with six and a half feet of gorgeous sexy male so close beside her.

'A good time? What on earth does that have to do with our trip?'

'A lot.' To Kaitlin's surprise, he added, 'Have I told you that you're looking very beautiful?'

Kaitlin tried to ignore the pleasure burgeoning within her like a furled bud opening up to the sun. 'You hadn't, but thanks.'

'You look great in that colour you're wearing.'

'It's called teal, and thanks again.'

Man-woman talk. And, despite her better judgement, she was enjoying it.

Involuntarily, her gaze went to eyes warm with laughter, and to lips that tilted sensuously at the corners—how *good* they felt whenever they touched hers. From Flynn's face, her gaze moved to his shoulders, shoulders so broad that the most independent of women might think how wonderful it would be to let go of her problems for a time as she leaned her head against them; and then moved lower still to the expanse of muscled chest visible where the top buttons of his shirt were open, making that same woman dream of nuzzling her mouth against the tanned skin.

'What are you thinking, Kaitlin?'

'Private thoughts, cowboy,' she told him saucily.

'Care to share them?'

'They wouldn't be private then, would they?'

How easy it would be to fall in love with Flynn again, yet she dared not let it happen. One dose of heartbreak had been more than enough, making Kaitlin determined never to be so unhappy again. Five years ago she had been young and inexperienced, too naïve to understand that Flynn was just toying with her affections, that all he was interested in was physical gratification. She was older now, more cynical, hopefully wiser. More than anything, she was aware of Flynn's grand plan, and she had no intention of letting herself become a part of it.

Deliberately she turned from Flynn and looked down at the ranch. Flynn flew purposely low, so that she could get a better view.

'When was the last time you saw the range from up here, Kaitlin?'

Her forehead puckered. 'I don't remember.'

'Gives you a different perspective, doesn't it?'

Kaitlin's head jerked around. 'Maybe so. And OK, maybe I do need more livestock and cowboys and pasture. But no matter how bad things are, I'll never let you have the ranch.'

'So you keep telling me.'

'I have every intention of putting the ranch back on its feet, Flynn.'

'If you say so.'

For a while things had been going better, but now the

mood had changed. Kaitlin had been *stupid* if she thought she could relax, even for a minute, when she was with Flynn.

'Turn the plane,' she ordered.

'Don't be silly.'

'There's no point in going on with this trip, Flynn.'

'I don't agree,' he said lazily.

'You know I can't stand the thought of going anywhere with you.'

Dark eyes searched her face. 'There's that mortgage payment,' he reminded her.

'Yes... But it's going to be an awful day, Flynn.'

'It doesn't have to be.'

'What do you mean?'

'I was going to suggest a truce.'

She stared at him disbelievingly. 'You've given up the idea of owning the ranch?'

Flynn grinned. 'You know better than that.'

'Then there can't be a truce,' she said tersely.

'There can—for today. I won't mention your payments, and you won't think about them.'

'You speak as if we're children, Flynn, but we're not.' Her voice was tight with tension. 'We're adults, and we both know you won't rest till you have what you want. So a truce can only be temporary.'

Flynn's laughter was seductive and disturbingly close to her ear. 'That's what a truce is, Kaitlin—temporary. But I still say we can let ourselves enjoy the day. How about it?'

She was so tempted to say yes. Though the ranch was her life, it was very nice to think of escaping the chores, the loneliness and the monotony of routine for a day. It would be sheer bliss to forget her problems for a few hours; to enjoy the sights and sounds of the city, and have fun spending someone else's money. *To let herself enjoy Flynn's company—just this once.*

'What do you say, Kaitlin?'

'You seem to forget,' she said slowly, 'that you only wanted me to come with you because I'm a rich bitch who knows her way around clothing stores.'

Once more, the dark eyes sparkled. 'Part of that description was yours, not mine, Kaitlin.'

'You made your feelings pretty clear, Flynn. Besides, have you forgotten that my only reason for going with you is to perform a service?'

The expression in the rugged face was enigmatic. 'I've forgotten nothing. *Will* you let yourself enjoy the day?'

It was difficult to keep a cool head when Flynn was so near her. Muscled legs were just inches from Kaitlin's, and a tanned arm brushed seductively against her bare skin.

'Will you, Kaitlin?'

Kaitlin opened her mouth to say 'no.' But the word that emerged was, 'OK.'

She jerked when Flynn touched her knee. 'It will be a nice day, Kaitlin.'

She shifted restlessly in her seat, her knee burning beneath Flynn's fingers. 'Maybe…'

Flynn returned his hand to the controls, and Kaitlin's eyes followed it. It was a large hand, well-shaped, roughened by years of work. A very beautiful male hand, Kaitlin thought. Without meaning to, she found herself remembering how it used to feel on the soft secret parts of her body. Involuntarily, she shivered.

'Cold?' Flynn asked.

'No.'

'I have a sweater somewhere.'

'Thanks, but I don't need it.'

Flynn shot her an enigmatic glance, but she turned away from the all-too-perceptive eyes, and looked through the side window over the endless prairie landscape.

They were landing in Austin when Kaitlin said, 'I need some time alone before we start shopping.'

'I guessed as much.'

She turned her head to look at Flynn. 'Spoken as if you know.'

'That you want to see Bill Seally?' He laughed at her startled expression. 'That is where you're off to, isn't it?'

'Yes,' Kaitlin said, and hoped he was unable to read all her other thoughts as easily.

'I've been wondering,' Flynn said, 'whether you've spoken to Bill at all since I took over the mortgage.'

'No, though not for want of trying. I've called several times, but I can never get him. In fact, I spoke to Anne before we left this morning, and as usual Bill wasn't in.'

'Can't say I'm surprised.'

'I never had any difficulty getting hold of him before now,' Kaitlin said grimly.

'Did you let Anne know you were coming?'

'No…'

'In that case, I'll bet you'll find Bill this time,' Flynn said.

Bill Seally owned several stores in Austin, and without speaking to his wife again Kaitlin might have been hard-pressed to know where to find him. But Kaitlin was aware that Bill had always retained a special affection for his hardware store, the first of many businesses he had established, and she decided to go there first.

She saw him immediately. Bill Seally, rich enough to employ a host of employees to look after his various concerns, was still a salesman at heart. Through the years, she had often heard him telling her father, he had never lost his pleasure in face-to-face dealings with his customers.

He was behind the counter now, joking with a man as he wrapped his purchases. He had not noticed Kaitlin's arrival, so she was able to watch him a few seconds unobserved. It was only when she stepped forward, away from the store's entrance, that Bill saw her. In an instant the laughter died on his lips.

'Why, Kaitlin…' The customer momentarily forgotten, Bill took a step backwards.

Kaitlin forced a smile. 'Hi there, Bill. I'm in no hurry, please don't stop what you're doing.'

'Yes… I mean no.'

He returned to the customer, but did not finish his joke. Bill looked flustered, Kaitlin thought.

When the man had gone, Bill walked around the counter. 'Kaitlin, honey, what a nice surprise.'

'A surprise,' she agreed quietly, 'but somehow I don't think it's a nice one.'

'How can you say that?' Bill's expression was pained. 'Why, you're family—almost. I can't remember a time when your parents weren't a part of our lives. Anne and I and your parents…our dearest friends. And now you… How are you doing, honey?'

'How do you think I'm doing, Bill?'

His eyes met hers a second, then shifted away. 'I guess things aren't easy,' he muttered.

'No, they aren't. Why didn't you tell me, Bill?'

'Kaitlin… You're referring to the mortgage.'

'Why didn't you tell me you'd ceded it to Flynn?'

'Kaitlin… Honey… You have to understand… Business isn't that good… It was months since you'd made any payments. And…' He stopped. 'Look, Kaitlin, I'm your friend, never doubt that. But Anne and I have to think of ourselves.'

'I never expected you to subsidize me, Bill, and I don't blame you for making other arrangements. Really, I don't. I guess, I just… Well, I suppose I thought it would be OK if it took a little longer for me to put things right. I should have known I was wrong.'

Bill looked relieved. 'I knew you'd understand.'

'I just wish you'd told me how you felt about things. Maybe there would have been a way… Maybe I could have raised a loan through a bank.'

'Maybe,' he said unhappily.

'I… I just wish you'd told me about Flynn.'

Bill met her eyes. 'Would it have made a difference?'

Kaitlin studied the face of her father's best and oldest friend, a face she had known all her life. How odd it was that she had never before noticed how weak that face was.

'It would have made a difference,' she said quietly. 'Can you imagine my shock when Flynn walked in—actually he didn't walk, he landed his plane on the airstrip—and told me that he had taken over the mortgage. At least, if I'd known, I'd have been prepared.'

Once more the older man's gaze left hers, and his eyelids began a nervous flickering. 'I meant to tell you, Kaitlin.

Should have… Things were so hectic, I didn't get around to it. But I did mean to tell you. Honestly.'

Bill was not telling her the truth, Kaitlin knew. For the first time she understood that Bill Seally was a coward.

'I have to go,' she said.

'Really?' He did not succeed in masking his relief.

'Goodbye, Bill,' Kaitlin said, and wondered if her parents' friend understood the finality of the farewell.

Flynn was there before her in the store where they'd arranged to meet. He came towards her, a tall figure, big and tough and overwhelmingly masculine. A man a woman could love—in different circumstances.

'Hi, Kaitlin. Find Bill? Speak to him?'

'Yes.'

'You weren't gone long.'

'There wasn't much to say.'

He looked down at her, dark eyes penetrating and perceptive. 'I did try to warn you.'

'I know you did.'

He looked at her a moment longer. Then he said, 'I guess we should start looking at clothes.'

'I'm ready.'

'On second thoughts, let's have something to eat first.'

Abruptly, Kaitlin said, 'Thanks, Flynn, but as I've told you before, I don't need your pity.'

'Who said anything about pity? I'm hungry, I could do with a good steak.'

'Flynn—'

He grinned at her. 'Humour me, Kaitlin.'

They found a steak-house on the next corner. When their food had been put in front of them—steak, French fries and a crisp salad—Flynn looked at Kaitlin. 'Tell me about your meeting with Bill Seally.'

'Not much to tell,' Kaitlin said slowly.

'It didn't go well?'

'No worse than I should have expected.'

'Tell me about it.'

Flynn didn't interrupt Kaitlin as she talked about her disappointment at Bill's behaviour, her hurt and her sense of betrayal.

'Perhaps it's as well you saw him, Kaitlin,' he said, when she had finished.

'It's not easy to discover you've been let down by a person you cared for and trusted.'

'I've learned that.'

Kaitlin looked at him questioningly. 'Thinking of someone in particular?'

'I am.' His tone was hard.

'Were you badly hurt, Flynn?'

His eyes flicked her face. 'You could say that.'

Who had hurt this man, Kaitlin wondered. His wife, Elise? Someone else? Flynn had a closed expression that stopped her from asking the question. For a while they ate in silence.

When they did talk once more, Kaitlin saw that Flynn's mood had changed again. The hardness left his face as he told her about the rodeo circuit: the excitement and the danger, the rivalry and the companionship.

'It's a unique kind of world,' Flynn said.

'Even as a spectator—and that's all I've ever been—I've seen that.' It was not the first time they had talked about Flynn's rodeo days, yet Kaitlin hung on his every word.

'As a spectator you only see what goes on in the arena.'

'I know that.'

As if from nowhere, an amazing thought came to Kaitlin's mind. Startled, she stared at Flynn. But, no, the idea was impossible. Nevertheless, she asked the question. 'How about women?'

'There are always women on the circuit. I've told you about them, Kaitlin. The fans. The groupies. Women like my wife, like Elise.'

'I'm thinking of the cowgirls. The women who participate in rodeo events.'

'They do their stunts, just as the men do.'

'Are their winnings good?'

'The best women earn well.' He stopped, and looked at her suspiciously. 'Why the questions, Kaitlin? Don't tell me you're thinking of trying the circuit?'

Kaitlin laughed. 'Good heavens, Flynn!'

'Are you?' he demanded.

'Can't a girl talk?'

'As long as that's all it is.'

'Why would you care anyway? Other women participate—if I wanted to, what would be wrong with it?'

'It's dangerous,' he said shortly. 'You could get hurt.'

Something made her say, 'I wouldn't have thought that would worry you.'

She sat very still as brooding eyes swept her face. 'What makes you say that?'

Kaitlin shrugged. 'You hold my mortgage. If I was hurt, it would be easier for you to take over the ranch.'

The brooding look vanished as Flynn grinned at her. 'Now there's a thought.'

'Am I right?'

Reaching across the table, Flynn put a hand over hers. 'No, Kaitlin, you couldn't be more wrong. It's true I want the ranch, but not at the cost of an accident. So in case you have any silly ideas about entering a rodeo, forget them.'

The big hand on hers was sending shock waves of desire rocking through her system. 'We were talking about rodeos, and it was just a question,' she said unsteadily.

'As long as that's all it was.' His hand left hers. 'What will you have for dessert?'

'I've eaten all I can.'

Flynn's grin turned wicked. 'I haven't. In fact, I have this enormous craving for ice-cream, and I won't enjoy it nearly as much if I have to eat alone.'

It was easy to smile back at him. 'I'll have one too in that case.'

Looking across the table at Flynn, Kaitlin thought how different he was from Bill Seally. Where Bill was weak, Flynn was all rugged toughness and strength. It would not occur to Flynn to avoid doing something just because it was difficult or unpleasant. With Flynn Henderson a woman would always know where she stood.

'Penny for your thoughts,' he said.

'I don't think so.'

'More than that?'

She shot him a cheeky grin. 'More than even you could afford.'

She would never tell him that she had just decided there couldn't be a man in all of Texas who could compare with him. Not a man who could be as attractive as Flynn, certainly not as sexy. Not a man she would ever love as she loved him.

Love! Kaitlin gave a muffled gasp. She had tried so hard not to let herself fall in love with Flynn again. Only this morning she had resolved not to let her feelings get the better of her. Why hadn't she realized that it was already too late? She had been in love with Flynn five years ago, and she was still in love with him now. Was it possible, she wondered despairingly, that she had never stopped loving him?

'Something wrong, Kaitlin?' he asked curiously.

She gave her head a violent shake. 'Not a thing.' If Flynn were to discover her feelings, he would use the knowledge to further his grand plan, and she could not bear it if he did that. *He must not know that she was in love with him.*

'Kaitlin—'

'It's nothing.' Her throat was tight with nerves. 'I hope the waiter hurries with the ice-cream, or we won't get much shopping done.'

'Take a look at this jacket. And this one... Oh, and Flynn, here's a really nice shirt, I think you should try it on. And ties. *No*—!' giggling '—not *that* tie, not with these clothes!'

'Why not, Kaitlin?'

'It's dead wrong.'

'Really?'

'The colours—so gaudy.'

'I wouldn't have known.'

Kaitlin was laughing as she looked at Flynn. 'You're teasing, you must be. I know you don't need me to tell you the tie is wrong.'

'I'm just a simple cowboy, Kaitlin. What do I know about jackets and ties?'

She shook her head. 'You haven't been a simple cowboy

for ages, and I believe you know more than you're letting on.'

'You're wrong,' Flynn insisted. 'Show me jeans and boots and Stetsons, and I know what I want. Formal clothes are a mystery to me.'

'After years in the oil business?'

'Not many years, Kaitlin, and mostly out in the oilfields. I can count on one hand the times I've set foot in a corporate boardroom. At heart I'll always be a cowboy, happiest when I'm on a ranch. I'm not a suit and tie person, Kaitlin, never have been. Which is why your services are so valuable to me.'

She looked at him curiously. 'So valuable that they're worth half a mortgage payment?'

'Worth every cent.'

'I think you're making fun of me, Flynn Henderson.'

'Now, Kaitlin Mullins, why would I do that?' But his eyes were sparkling.

'Because despite being ruthless, you're also a tease.'

'Am I ruthless, Kaitlin?'

Looking up into the tough face with its hard lines and angles, Kaitlin said slowly, 'Ruthless? Yes, I think so. You'd think nothing of foreclosing on my mortgage.'

He did not contradict her, but said instead, 'And the part about being a tease?'

'You were always a tease, Flynn. You used to enjoy a joke.'

'I still do.'

He was smiling at her. His lips, surprisingly sensuous lips in such an uncompromisingly masculine face, were tilted at the corners, and his eyes shone with a roguish gleam. Kaitlin experienced a great urge to go to Flynn, right there in the middle of the store, to put her arms around his waist and her head against the rock-hard chest, but she knew better than to do it. This was no time for romantic folly: she was here for a purpose, and she'd best keep that in mind every minute.

'Getting back to your clothes,' she said briskly.

'My clothes. Right. Funny how we keep forgetting them.'

'I haven't forgotten them once, Flynn.'

'That's my girl.' He was laughing at her once more.

'I'm not your girl,' she said, pretending to be cross. 'OK, Flynn, so you want to impress the big shots in the oil business. Apart from a jacket and trousers, do you think you might need a suit?'

'You're the one who's supposed to be doing all the thinking today, Kaitlin.'

'As long as you understand that I'm no expert when it comes to men's clothes.'

'Fit me out and I'll be eternally grateful to you.'

Flynn was teasing again, Kaitlin knew, but she was loving every moment. Suddenly they were both laughing, a together kind of laughter, and Kaitlin thought how *good* that was: the kind of laughter that could be a part of everyday life, of a shared life. But that could never be, not for them. Firmly, she steered her mind back to the matter in hand.

A salesman picked up the clothes they had taken from the racks, and said, 'I'll put these things in a fitting room. Are you ready to try on, sir?' And with a look at Kaitlin, 'If the lady would like to come, too?'

When the man was out of earshot, Kaitlin said, 'I'm not going to the fitting-room with you, Flynn.'

'I want you to.'

'No, Flynn, that was never part of the deal.'

'It is now.' From one moment to the next, the laughing tone had taken on the sound of unquestionable authority. The implication of Flynn's words was clear: don't forget you're being well rewarded.

Abruptly, Kaitlin said, 'OK, if I must. Let's go and get this over with.'

Reluctantly, she followed him into the fitting-room. A wicked look from Flynn told her that he knew just how uneasy she felt. The curtained area seemed smaller than it really was with Flynn's particular brand of maleness dominating its space. A feverish Kaitlin felt as if the very air vibrated with his raw sexiness.

Restlessly, she said, 'Why don't I wait outside while you get changed?'

Flynn shot her a sparkling look. 'Why would you do that? There's room for both of us here. Unless, of course, you're scared that the sight of my bare chest will offend you?'

Actually Kaitlin was imagining how aroused she would be, and how difficult it would be to keep from throwing herself into Flynn's arms.

'I want you to stay,' he told her, his eyes holding hers as he began to unbutton his shirt.

Kaitlin tried very hard to keep her gaze averted, but, as if her eyes were propelled by something stronger than her own will, she found herself staring longingly at a bronzed chest.

'Well?' Flynn asked at last.

Kaitlin, who was trying to deal with the sensations he had aroused in her, looked at him through dazed eyes. 'Well, what?'

'What do you think?'

That you're the sexiest man alive. That I'll never be able to love anyone else.

'Are any of these things right for me, Kaitlin? The jacket, the shirt, the tie?'

Until that moment, she hadn't given a thought to his clothes. 'I'm not sure,' she murmured.

'You have to be sure, Kaitlin. That's why you're here.'

Her mind was a whirl of conflicting emotions, and yet she knew she must concentrate, somehow. 'The thing is—' Kaitlin made her voice brisk '—so much depends on your image.'

'Do I have one?'

'Everyone does.' It was becoming a little easier to speak normally. 'There are the conservative dressers and the trendy ones. The wealthy oilmen who only wear the most expensive clothes, and the more laid-back types who go for more casual styles.'

'How do you see me, Kaitlin?'

'Hm—' she pretended to think '—are you the conservative type or are you more trendy? Or are you just a great hunk of a cowboy wearing formal clothes under protest?'

Flynn was laughing. 'You mean you don't know, Kaitlin?'

'I'm considering.'

'Let's see if I can help you,' Flynn said.

Kaitlin watched in amusement as he selected an elegant grey tie patterned with discreet narrow stripes. He combed his hair neatly sideways, and put a small strip of black paper under his nose, holding it in place with his upper lip so that the paper looked like a moustache.

'My image?' Flynn asked through his teeth.

Kaitlin burst out laughing. 'Ultra conservative. Oilman deluxe.'

'Will you entrust your millions to me, madame?'

She was laughing so hard that she could hardly speak. 'Every one of my countless millions.'

'Not so fast, madame. Not so fast.'

Dropping the paper from his lip, Flynn replaced the grey tie with one that was festooned with bright pictures of women and flowers. He used his hands to push his hips aggressively forwards.

'Hey, little lady, how 'bout lettin' me look after your money now?'

Kaitlin was still laughing. 'If you had a microphone, you'd pass for a rock musician. Not a chance I'd hand you my millions.'

'You don't care for my image?'

'It's not conducive to the oil business.'

'Hm. What would you call it?'

'Offbeat.'

'Offbeat? Well, what do you know.'

Lastly, he put on his Stetson and shoved his hands deep in his trouser pockets. 'Now?'

Her heart gave a funny little thud against her ribs. 'Now you're a cowboy. Flynn, you should have been an actor.'

'Think so?'

'You're marvellous!'

Flynn looked down at her a long moment. At last he said, 'I like you like this, Kaitlin.'

'What do you mean?'

'Laughing. Carefree. This is the way you were meant to be.'

'Yes,' she said. And then, 'If only…'

'If only what?'

The laughter left her face as she stared at him, appalled at the words that had so nearly escaped her. *If only it could always be like this. You and me, laughing and happy. Together.* For a few minutes she had actually forgotten why she was here with Flynn. She had allowed herself to behave as if theirs was a normal man-woman relationship.

'If only *what*, Kaitlin?' he asked intently.

'Forget I said that.'

'I want to know.' There was an odd urgency in Flynn's expression.

Kaitlin glanced at her watch. 'We should start making some choices.'

'In a minute.'

Giving her no time to move away from him, Flynn slung a tie around her waist, capturing her and pulling her to him.

'Don't,' she said.

'You were about to say something, and then, for some reason, you thought better of it.'

'Flynn…'

'Did it concern the two of us, Kaitlin?'

'Even if it did…'

He drew her closer, so close that she could feel the hard muscles of his legs pressing against her. Kaitlin felt weak.

'Don't you think I deserve to know what you were going to say, Kaitlin?'

She loved him deeply, fervently, with a passion that surpassed the emotions she'd experienced five years earlier. But he did not love her, and so she couldn't tell him what he wanted to know. She made a conscious effort not to let her body arch against him.

'The salesman,' she whispered. 'What would he think?'

'Does it matter?' Flynn responded impatiently.

'He could walk in at any moment.'

'If he did, he'd take us for a loving couple.' Flynn was so close to Kaitlin that when he spoke his breath was warm on her face.

'Which we're not,' she said with some difficulty. She made herself look at him. 'We're playing a dangerous game, Flynn.'

'Are we?'

'Acting the part of a loving couple, when we're not.'

His eyes held hers, defying them to move away. 'What's dangerous about it?'

'If we're not very careful we might end up believing the game.'

His eyes narrowed. 'You used to enjoy games, Kaitlin.'

Kaitlin's throat was tight. 'I don't care for this one. We both know the reason I'm here with you.'

'I believe,' Flynn said, in a voice that was almost un-nervingly soft, 'that for a while you forgot the reason.'

'You could be right.' It was a struggle to keep the jerk-iness out of her own voice. 'But I shouldn't have forgotten. What we're doing here today is business, Flynn. Only busi-ness. A matter of a mortgage and services rendered. It's a mistake to confuse it with anything else.'

'If you say so.' A coolness had crept into his tone.

She kept her own tone crisp. 'Do you like any of these things, Flynn, or would you rather look elsewhere?'

But Flynn, it seemed, had had enough of trying on clothes. Together they decided on a grey suit, teaming it with a white shirt and a subtly patterned tie; and a navy sports jacket, dark brown pants and a few more ties.

'That's it then,' Kaitlin said, when they had made their choices.

She was about to leave the fitting-room when Flynn said, 'I need something formal, as well.'

'More formal than the things we've already chosen?'

'There's going to be a banquet, Kaitlin, and the invitation calls for a black tie.'

She shot him a look of surprise. 'A banquet, Flynn? First time you've mentioned it.'

'Dancing afterwards.'

Dancing… Unbidden, a picture appeared in Kaitlin's mind: Flynn with a woman in his arms. She was unprepared for the stab of pain the picture brought with it.

Carefully, she asked, 'Are you asking me to help you choose a tuxedo?'

Dark eyes gleamed. 'Is there a problem with that?'

Kaitlin would have liked nothing better than to tell Flynn Henderson to choose his own banquet clothes, but there was still the question of the mortgage payment and the service she'd agreed to perform. There was nothing for it but to grit her teeth and get on with the job.

Her heart did a funny little somersault when she saw Flynn in a tuxedo. With his broad chest and shoulders filling the jacket, and the crisp white shirt emphasizing his tan, he was more handsome than any man had a right to be.

'What do you think, Kaitlin?'

She made herself meet his gaze. 'You'll pass muster with the oilmen.'

'And the women?'

'What about the women, Flynn?'

'I told you, there'll be dancing.'

Every woman at the banquet would be dying for a turn in his arms.

'I dare say,' she said drily, 'the women won't reject you.'

'Well, that's a relief.' Flynn's laughter, so close to her ears, had the sound of a taunt.

Kaitlin was glad when they left the store at last. When Flynn suggested another meal, she thanked him but shook her head.

'Not at all hungry, Kaitlin?'

'No.'

'Something bothering you?'

'Should there be?'

'You were in such a good mood for a while. Around the time we started looking at tuxedos things seemed to change.'

He was far too perceptive. But she knew that already.

She managed a deliberately brisk look. 'It's been a long day.'

'Nothing like the hours you usually work. You'll be telling me next that you're anxious to get back to the ranch.'

'As a matter of fact, I am.'

His eyes lingered on her face. 'I see.'

What exactly he saw, Kaitlin didn't know. But she was glad that he didn't question her further. They flew back to the ranch in silence.

When Flynn had landed the plane, he turned to Kaitlin. 'What you did today takes care of half of next week's payment. Think you'll be able to manage the one after that?'

'I hope so.'

'You don't sound at all certain.'

Reluctantly, Kaitlin said, 'I'll do my best to have the money for you on time.'

'I have a suggestion, Kaitlin.'

'Another service?' she asked warily.

'You're far better at choosing clothes than I'll ever be. If you don't think you'll have the money, there's something else you can do for me.'

'What's it this time?' Without knowing quite why, Kaitlin felt tense.

'More shopping.'

'Clothes again?'

'For a woman this time.'

Feeling a little ill, Kaitlin said, 'What kind of clothes? And who is the woman?'

'My date for the banquet.'

'Your date…' Kaitlin hoped she wouldn't choke over the bitter taste in her mouth.

'My date, right. She's going to need fitting out too.' Flynn's tone was light, as if he was unaware of Kaitlin's distress.

'Doesn't she have clothes already?' Kaitlin made herself ask.

'Sure, she does. But she'll need something formal. Do you call that kind of dress a gown?'

Kaitlin stared at Flynn in stunned disbelief. 'I couldn't have heard you right—you want *me* to choose it?'

'Precisely.'

Deep inside her, mixed with Kaitlin's pain, a fierce anger was beginning to stir. 'That's ridiculous, Flynn! I'm sure the woman, whoever she is, is quite capable of buying her own gown.'

'I want to buy it for her.'

'*Why*?'

Airily, Flynn said, 'I have my reasons.'

'What a surprise that will be for her.'

'A nice one, I hope.'

'Don't bet on it, Flynn!' Kaitlin said grimly. 'I don't think the woman exists who wants someone else to buy clothes for her. She'd probably hate my choice anyway.'

'Oh, I don't know, Kaitlin. If today was anything to go by, I'd say you have excellent taste.'

'Women's tastes differ.' Her lips were stiff, her throat dry with unhappiness. 'I might like a dress that she'll hate.'

Flynn's grin was wicked. 'Let that be my problem.'

A new thought occurred to Kaitlin. 'Besides which, how can I possibly buy for someone else? I don't know her size.'

Flynn's eyes moved assessingly over her body. 'If it fits you, it will fit her.'

'Take your…your woman…and let her do her own shopping, Flynn.'

But he was unyielding. 'I want you to come with me.'

'No, Flynn.'

'Why not?'

'I don't want to.'

Dark eyes raked her face. 'Is it possible you're jealous, Kaitlin?' came the insolently drawled question.

'*Jealous*!' The word burst like a pistol shot from her lips. 'Why on earth would I be jealous, Flynn Henderson?'

'Just wondered.'

'Well, you can stop wondering! Since I couldn't care less who you associate with, there's absolutely no reason why I'd be jealous.'

'Good. Then you'll come.'

'No, I will not! Helping you choose clothes for yourself was one thing, but this is one assignment I don't fancy.'

'I want you to come, Kaitlin.'

Golly, but the man was persistent.

'If I refuse?' she asked tensely.

'In that case,' Flynn said cheerfully, 'I hope you'll manage to come up with the money for your mortgage.'

CHAPTER SEVEN

THE phone rang a week later. 'Hello, Kaitlin.'

'Hi, Flynn,' she made herself say briskly.

'How are you?'

Clutching the receiver, Kaitlin closed her eyes briefly. In the days since the shopping trip, one thought had never left her mind: *Flynn had a woman in his life.*

Behind her lids she could see him now, every inch of him imprinted on her mind as sharply as if she was looking at a photo. Day after day she agonized over the fact that she had allowed herself to fall in love with him all over again. But now was not the time to think of that. She must be alert to whatever Flynn was about to ask of her. Flynn Henderson, her adversary.

'I'm great,' she said. 'Never better.'

'Ranch doing OK?'

'The ranch is great, too. Why are you calling, Flynn?'

'To say hi?' he suggested laconically.

'I don't believe that for a moment.'

'People do that, Kaitlin.'

'Other people. Not you, Flynn. I never hear from you unless you want something.'

He chuckled. 'Bad as that, Kaitlin?'

'Worse,' she said grimly. 'Why did you call, Flynn? The real reason.'

'I think you know.' His voice was matter-of-fact now.

She did know, of course, but for some reason his call had taken her by surprise. It shocked her to realize that she was trembling. Before the phone call went much further, she needed to regain some measure of control.

'I do know,' she acknowledged reluctantly.

'The rest of that mortgage payment is due at the end of the week, Kaitlin. Will you be able to pay?'

'Flynn… Flynn, you have to understand… I was hoping I'd be able to pay, but I can't. I need time.'

'I'm afraid not, Kaitlin.'

She swallowed hard. 'Have you any idea how hard it is for me to plead?'

'You don't have to do that. There's an alternative to money. Last week you were quite happy to perform a service for half the payment.'

Last week she hadn't been choosing banquet clothes for some other woman.

'You already know what I want you to do for me, Kaitlin.'

'A gown,' she said, trying to keep the bitterness from her tone. 'You want me to help you choose a gown for your friend.'

'I knew you'd remember.'

'What if I refuse?'

'Then you leave me no alternative, Kaitlin.'

That night Kaitlin sat at her dressing-table, looking down at her grandmother's pride and joy, a wooden box with a pretty hand-carved inlay. At last, slowly, reluctantly, she turned the old-fashioned key.

Inside the box, on a bed of blue velvet, lay the ring which her grandmother had given her on her sixteenth birthday. It was a lovely piece of antique jewellery, with a pearl at its centre and tiny diamonds around the edges.

Kaitlin could still hear her grandmother's words. 'Your grandfather gave this to me the day we were married. You're too young to wear it now, but I hope you'll enjoy it when you're older, Katie.'

'I'll cherish it forever,' she had told the beloved old lady, who had died not long afterwards.

Forever…

Her fingers trembled as she took the ring from the box and slid it onto the fourth finger of her right hand. 'Darling Gran,' she thought, 'what would you think of the mess I've gotten myself into?'

In a few days Flynn would be back at the ranch, expecting payment. The easy thing would be to go on another shopping trip with him—Kaitlin, the rich bitch who would know just the right gown to select for the lady love who was going to accompany Flynn to the banquet.

But she couldn't do it. Flynn was asking too damned much of her. Quite apart from the woman in his life— Kaitlin loathed her without knowing anything about her— she could not allow herself to dance to Flynn's whims: not if she valued her independence and her pride, which she did. Flynn was playing a game with her, and she could not let him get away with it.

The problem was she had no ready cash. There was only the ring, her precious ring, and the hope that it would bring in enough money to tide her over for a while.

'Forgive me, Gran, but I think if you were alive you'd understand that I have to do this.' Kaitlin whispered the words softly in the silent, empty room.

Next morning, very early, after giving instructions to the men, Kaitlin left the ranch in a truck. She did not say where she was going, only that she would not be back until late the next day.

Kaitlin wished she had thought of loading her camera with new film before Flynn arrived at the ranch for her payment; confident, self-assured, he seemed to take it for granted that she would be ready for the trip into town.

His eyes narrowed as she handed him the envelope. 'What is this?'

Kaitlin suppressed a smile. 'What do you think?'

He opened the envelope and drew out the cheque. *'I'll be darned*!' His face was a picture of amazement.

Kaitlin's visit to the pawnshop had been an unpleasant experience, with the pawnbroker driving a hard bargain. Kaitlin had had to swallow back the tears that threatened to spill as she handed over the ring to him. At least, Flynn's astonished expression went some way towards making up for the anguish of giving up her beloved heirloom, and the embarrassment she had suffered.

'Why so surprised, Flynn?' Kaitlin asked saucily. 'Isn't this what you came for?'

'You know darn well what I came for. I thought you and I were going to town together.'

'Sorry to disappoint you.' She knew she didn't sound in the least bit sorry.

'Where did you get this money, Kaitlin?' he demanded.

She lifted her chin at him. 'You have your payment—that's all that concerns you.'

In an instant, he had closed the distance between them. 'What've you been up to, Kaitlin?' he growled, as he seized her shoulders in his big hands.

'Up to?' she repeated, trying to hide the excitement that coursed through her at his touch.

'You heard me.'

'Well, let's see—did I rob a gas station or a bank? Let me think... No... No, it wasn't that.'

'Where did this money come from, Kaitlin?'

'I'm a rancher,' she reminded him.

'With no cattle to sell.'

'You don't know that, Flynn Henderson.'

'There are things I know.'

'How could I forget? The great Flynn Henderson always knows everything. Just as he knew the exact moment when my ranch would be ripe for take-over. Well, Flynn, this time you seem to be misinformed.'

'So you're not going to tell me where you got the money.' His eyes were steel-hard.

'Spot on, Flynn. Full marks for understanding.'

They gazed at each other a few moments: the deliberately provocative, sparkling-eyed girl and the ruggedly attractive man. His hands tightened on her shoulders. As he drew her towards him there was a heart-stopping moment when Kaitlin wondered if he was going to kiss her. Instead, he let her go.

'What about your next payment, Kaitlin?'

'No need to worry about that today,' she told him, as airily as she could.

She watched him leave, smiling to herself as the plane rose in the air. She was exuberant, elated. True, another payment was due very soon, and for the life of her she didn't know how she was going to make it. But she would worry about that in due course. Today she would just enjoy the satisfaction of knowing that, for once, she had got the better of Flynn.

Kaitlin had no money to meet the next payment. There were cattle she was hoping to sell, but they were not yet ready for market, and she had nothing else of value that she could sell instead. This time there was nothing for it but to agree to accompany Flynn on the trip to town.

As before, he came for her in his plane. This time, however, she did not enjoy flying with him. Always, at the back of Kaitlin's mind, was the unknown woman.

They were almost in Austin when she said, 'This woman, this friend of yours, do you realize that I know nothing about her? I can't imagine how I'll go about finding something she'll like.'

Flynn was smiling as he turned to look at her. 'I have confidence in you.'

'Don't be so certain.'

'Why don't you trust your own taste, Kaitlin? If you see a gown you like, chances are she will too.'

'Spoken like a man,' she said crossly. 'If all women had the same taste in clothing, there wouldn't be so many different styles and colours.'

'Point taken, but I still say, choose something you like.'

'It isn't that easy, Flynn. What's her colouring?'

'Blond.'

'Eyes?'

'Hm, let me think... I'd say they're probably green.'

'Same colouring as mine.'

'Come to think of it, yes.'

Kaitlin clenched her hands so tightly that her nails bit into the soft skin of her palms. At last she asked the question that had been on her mind from the moment she'd heard about the other woman.

'Is she pretty?'

'Very.' The answer came so quickly, it was clear Flynn

had not had to think about it. 'Actually,' he added, 'she's quite lovely.'

'Oh…' Kaitlin tried to ignore the pain that wrenched inside her.

Pleasantly, Flynn said, 'Anything else you want to know about my friend?'

'No. Well, yes… What is her name?'

'That,' he told her, 'isn't important. All I'm asking of you, Kaitlin, is that you help me buy her a beautiful dress. You don't need her name to do that.'

Flynn took Kaitlin to one of the most expensive boutiques in the city. The boutique's exterior—the gold lettering on the polished wooden door, the single beautiful gown in the window—was enough to hint at exclusivity.

On the sidewalk, Kaitlin stopped. '*This* is where we're going?' she asked in astonishment.

'You don't think you'll find something you'll like here?'

'Something your girlfriend will like,' Kaitlin corrected him matter-of-factly. 'Oh, yes, Flynn, there'll be something here.'

'Even if you don't find anything, hopefully this will be a good place to start looking.'

Every time Kaitlin saw Flynn, he surprised her anew. Intrigued, she asked, 'How on earth did you know about this place?'

Dark eyes sparkled down at her. 'Not your idea of a cowboy's hide-out?'

'Not quite. How did you know, Flynn?'

'Same way as I learn things about the oil business,' he told her. 'I made it my business to find out about it.'

Obviously, only the best was good enough for Flynn's girlfriend, Kaitlin thought enviously, as they walked into the boutique. Her envy was not for the material things that Flynn could give to the woman, only for the fact that he cared about her so much that he wanted to give her something exquisite. She must mean very much to him, came the painful thought.

They were greeted by a saleswoman who was beautifully

clad and coiffed. Beneath her carefully welcoming smile lurked an expression of disdain, as if cowboys in Stetsons were a rarity in her domain, and not at all welcome. The disdain lasted only as long as it took for Flynn to smile at her, and then the unpleasant expression was replaced by an adoring look. He has her eating out of his hand, Kaitlin thought wryly. No new experience for him, surely—his cowboy toughness coupled with his sexy charisma made for a combination few women would be able to resist.

In no time they were being shown one beautiful dress after another. Designer gowns, the saleswoman assured Kaitlin, each dress one of a kind: nobody would arrive at the banquet in a gown like hers. Kaitlin did not think it necessary to tell the woman that she would neither be wearing the dress nor going to the banquet.

One gown was lovelier than all the rest. A dream of a gown. A shimmering vision in green, the bodice was adorned with tiny pearls, and the sleeves were made of a delicate lace. Flynn insisted she try it on.

When he suggested going to the fitting-room with her, Kaitlin gave the idea very short shrift: there were some things that her services did not include, she told him firmly. Instead, she walked into the main area of the boutique, and modelled each dress in turn. The saleswoman, starry-eyed despite her sophistication, was never far from Flynn's side, and she bestowed lavish praise on each gown.

Flynn's own verbal comments were few. His eyes spoke for him instead; eyes which studied Kaitlin's slender body in gowns some of which left little to the imagination; eyes which heated Kaitlin's blood as they moved over her.

She had left the green gown for last. When she looked in the mirror, she couldn't believe what she was seeing. It looked as if it had been made for her, hugging the slender lines of her body, while at the same time revealing soft curves where she hadn't known she possessed any. The colour of the dress emphasized the colour of her eyes, so that they glowed like emeralds against her tanned skin. Kaitlin knew she had never looked more beautiful. If she could choose one material thing above all others, it would be to own this gown.

'Kaitlin.'

At the sound of her name, her head jerked. For a few minutes she had actually forgotten that Flynn was waiting for her on the other side of the fitting-room door. She had even forgotten—*how was that possible*?—that the gown could never be hers.

'Are you coming out, Kaitlin?'

'Yes…'

But for a long moment, Kaitlin stood motionless. There was a part of her that longed to let Flynn see her looking so beautiful. But there was another part, too, that did not want him to see her in the dress, not when it was meant for someone else.

A minute passed, and then Flynn called again. 'Kaitlin.'

'Yes.'

'You're taking a long time in there. Need some help?'

There was nothing for it. Slowly, with a mixture of shyness and eagerness, Kaitlin opened the fitting-room door.

'I was beginning to wonder whether…'

The words died away as Flynn looked at Kaitlin. An expression she had seen before appeared in his face. The expression made her shyer than ever: at the same time it made her very excited.

For a minute at least Flynn didn't say a word. Kaitlin stood before him, trying to hide an inner trembling as his eyes moved over her. Deep inside her, feelings were stirring: longing, hunger, a gnawing desire. She felt, all at once, intensely conscious of her femininity.

'The gown is just right for madame,' the saleswoman was saying, but Kaitlin barely heard her. Her eyes were solely on the tall man in the cowboy clothes.

Moistening her lips, she said, 'Flynn…' And when he still didn't speak, 'Do… Do you like it?'

'Like it?' His voice was husky.

'The gown? You… You haven't said whether you like it.'

His answer was to take her hand and direct her back towards the fitting-room.

'What are you doing?' she asked unsteadily.

'We're going to look at the dress—together.'

Earlier she had been able to refuse his suggestion that he join her in the fitting-room, but there was something between them now that had been missing then: a sensuousness filling the air, an invisible cord binding their linked hands, a sexual magnetism that was impossible to resist.

Numbly, Kaitlin let Flynn lead her where he wished, let him hold her shoulders, turning them in his hands until they were both facing the mirror. Her trembling had increased so much that she was certain he must feel it.

'Flynn....' Her eyes were not on the dress but on the image they created together: Flynn behind her, towering above her, with the top of her head just touching his chin; the rugged, broad-shouldered cowboy, and the fragile, delicate-featured girl.

'Flynn....' she said again.

'Do you have any idea how you look?' His voice was even huskier now.

'How?' she whispered.

'Beautiful.'

His lips touched her hair, but his eyes, dark and smouldering, never moved from hers in the mirror. Kaitlin could not have looked away from him had she tried—which she didn't. A fire was heating her body, she wanted nothing more than to turn around and go into his arms. At the same time, a small inner voice warned that she would regret what was happening.

Flynn's lips lifted from her hair. 'Beautiful,' he said again. 'So very beautiful.'

His hands dropped to her waist and circled it, two long fingers touching the soft underside of her breasts. In an instant, Kaitlin's nipples hardened.

'Don't,' she said in a strangled voice.

'Why not?'

'Someone could come in.'

'Nobody will come.'

'Flynn—'

The words she was about to say stuck in her throat as his arms tightened around her and he drew her against him. She could feel the hard length of his body against her back and her thighs, causing the inner fire to burn even more intensely. And all the while his eyes were still holding hers in the mirror.

After a minute or so his head dropped and he began to brush her throat with his lips. Up and down went his lips, and now his hands were moving over her, too, over her hips, and then up over her breasts.

Kaitlin's throat was so dry that it was growing more and more difficult to swallow. In the mirror, her eyes had a glazed look. She could not have said why, yet what was happening was more erotic than anything she had ever experienced.

After what seemed like eternity, Flynn's lips left her throat. Meeting her eyes once more, he said raggedly, 'You look even more beautiful than I imagined.'

'Flynn…'

'Shall we buy the dress, Kaitlin?'

'Yes!' The word emerged without thought.

It was a few seconds before reality struck her. Staring at the face above hers in the mirror, Kaitlin wondered how she could have let herself be so *stupid*.

Flynn must have seen the change in her expression. 'What's wrong, Kaitlin?'

Angrily, she said, 'Whether you buy the wretched dress or not, it's no concern of mine.'

'Isn't it?'

'No!' Really furious now, she spun around in his arms. 'You're forgetting something, aren't you, Flynn?'

'Am I?'

'You enjoy taunting me! Humiliating me!'

His eyes gleamed. 'Do I?'

'Yes, you do!' Pushing herself out of his hands, Kaitlin moved as far from Flynn as the confines of the fitting-room would allow. 'You know very well that this dress isn't for me, that it's for some other woman. Or had you really forgotten?'

Flynn laughed softly. 'I haven't forgotten a thing.'

So he had been playing with her all the time. Kaitlin could not remember when last she had felt quite so ill. Even her never-ending financial problems had never affected her quite so intensely.

'You really are a bastard, Flynn Henderson! Get out of here!'

'In a minute.'

'Now!'

His eyes glittered. 'What about the dress?'

'What about it?'

'Shall we buy it?'

'*We*? There's no *we* involved here. You need a dress for your girlfriend, Flynn. My sole function was to model it for you. I've done that. Whether you buy it is entirely up to you.'

'Wrong, Kaitlin. You didn't just come here today to model. You were also supposed to make some choices.'

Not this choice. Not with this dress. He could not ask it of her.

'This is one choice I can't make for you, Flynn.'

'You have to.' His tone was implacable.

'Bring your girlfriend to the store. She's going to the banquet. Let her try on the dress, let her tell you if she wants it.'

'I think *you* are forgetting something,' Flynn said smoothly. 'In exchange for quite a large amount of money, you are performing a service.'

Kaitlin felt chilled. 'You make me sound like a whore!'

'Aren't you being a bit melodramatic, Kaitlin? You agreed to go along with this.'

'I didn't have much alternative,' she muttered. Her throat felt dry as sandpaper.

Something came and went in Flynn's eyes. Compassion? No, Kaitlin thought, she must be imagining it: the new Flynn Henderson had no time for that kind of emotion.

And when he spoke, he was as unyielding as ever. 'The fact is, we do have an arrangement. So what's it to be, Kaitlin—do I buy the dress?'

Turning back to the mirror, Kaitlin took another look at herself. Pain tore through her at the very thought of some other woman in this achingly lovely garment. A woman who would be spending the evening—and maybe the night—in Flynn's arms.

'Do I buy it?' Flynn was relentless.

She could have said no, could have chosen one of the other dresses she had modelled for him. But Kaitlin had a great sense of integrity. For a while she had been so lost in the magic of the dress that she had actually forgotten it was meant for someone else. Flynn's cruel words had jerked her back to reality: she had promised a service in exchange for her mortgage payment, it was as simple as that. And although it was pure torment to imagine Flynn with another woman, she had to be honest.

Through dry lips she said, 'Go ahead and buy it.'

It was only when they were in Flynn's plane once more, and heading back to the ranch, that a furious Kaitlin said the words she had been wanting to say for hours.

'You're even more of a swine than I realized.'

'What's on your mind, Kaitlin?'

His look of amusement made her even angrier. 'As if you don't know!'

'Say it anyway.'

'The deal was that I'd help you buy a dress for your girl-friend. For you to get a few cheap sexual thrills from me at the same time was unforgivable. Only someone really rotten would stoop quite so low.'

'Correct me if I'm wrong,' Flynn drawled, 'but I got the feeling you were enjoying it, too.'

'How dare you!'

Flynn took his time about answering. Kaitlin tensed as she saw his gaze linger on her lips before moving to the rest of her body: a male look that was so blatant that she found herself trembling.

When he did speak, his tone was insolent. 'Remember, Kaitlin, I saw your eyes in the mirror. You were as eager as I was to make love. Either that, or you're a darn good actress.' And when Kaitlin didn't answer, 'Which was it? Did you hate it, or were you just acting?'

Deliberately, Kaitlin turned her head to the window, pretending an interest in the darkening brushlands far below them. When she was sure she could speak without crying, she said, 'I won't deny I was aroused.'

Flynn's exhalation was a small hiss. 'Well.'

'*Only at that moment*. Do you understand, Flynn? I was aroused only at the moment it was happening. The feeling didn't last—not when I realized the nasty game you were playing.'

'Certain it was a game, Kaitlin?'

'As certain as I can be,' she said bitterly. 'I wish it hadn't happened, but it did. Be that as it may, all I feel for you now is contempt.'

'I want you to come to the banquet with me.'

'*What*?' The word was torn from Kaitlin's throat.

'You heard me,' Flynn said.

Blindly Kaitlin gripped the receiver, glad that Flynn could not see her through the telephone line. The weeks since she had last seen him, had been sheer hell. Over and over again, mostly against her will, Kaitlin found herself reliving the scene in the boutique fitting-room, the memories refusing to fade.

Kaitlin—free-spirited, independent Kaitlin—had never imagined that loving a man could be anything like this. Nothing had prepared her for the longings that filled her mind during the day, that haunted her dreams at night. Flynn... She hungered for his kisses, she yearned to make love with him.

At the same time, she recognized the utter futility of her feelings, for she knew only too well that nothing had changed. Flynn had just one thing on his mind—his grand plan.

'What's this all about?' she demanded.

'I told you, I want you to come to the banquet with me.'

Kaitlin pushed her free hand through her hair. 'I don't understand...'

Even through the telephone line, his laughter was disturbingly seductive. 'I thought the question was simple. Will you come, Kaitlin?'

Kaitlin was outraged. 'You can't ask me that! You'd invited someone else, Flynn. What happened to your girlfriend? Did she have a change of mind? Did she ditch you?

The great Flynn Henderson let down by a woman, that must be a new experience for you. What happened, Flynn?'

'Why do you always need to make everything so complicated, Kaitlin?' he asked quietly. 'Why can't you just say a simple yes?'

'Because it isn't simple. You haven't told me what happened to the other woman.'

'It isn't important.'

'It is to me, Flynn. I don't like being a substitute. Why is your girlfriend not going to the banquet?'

'I told you,' he said, 'it isn't important.' Something in his voice made it clear he had no intention of saying more than that, however much she pressed him.

A few seconds passed. Then Flynn said, 'Isn't it enough that I want you to come with me?'

'No,' Kaitlin said.

She was about to put down the receiver, when Flynn spoke again. 'I'm sure you know your next payment is due soon.'

In Kaitlin's stomach, the muscles contracted into a hard knot of pain. Beads of perspiration formed on her upper lip and nervousness clogged her throat. 'Flynn…' she said.

'Will you be able to pay, Kaitlin?'

'I… I need time.'

'Your usual answer.'

'You'll have your payment.'

'When?'

'I'm hoping to sell some cattle.' In her own ears her tone sounded unconvincing.

'When will the sale take place?'

Damn Flynn for putting her on the spot like this! 'I'm not sure yet.'

'So the payment date will come and go because you don't know when you'll be making a sale.'

'Sooner or later—'

'It's clear you aren't a businesswoman,' he interrupted her. 'Sooner or later just isn't good enough in the business world, Kaitlin.'

'You don't understand—'

'I understand perfectly. You're not able to meet your

obligations, but you'd like to keep stringing me along just as you did Bill Seally. Well, I'm not Bill, and I won't wait.'

The hand that gripped the receiver was white-knuckled with tension. 'What are you saying, Flynn?'

'You know the answer, Kaitlin.'

She was suddenly very angry. 'This is another of your games, Flynn, and by now I know how much you're enjoying it. You don't seem to understand that it's no game for me. The life of my parents' ranch is at stake. The survival of my home. It means everything to me to keep things going for as long as I can.' She paused a minute, taking a breath, struggling for some semblance of control.

But when she went on her tone was still angry. 'You love having a hold over me, Flynn. You get a thrill out of making me dance to your wishes. It's blackmail, nothing less.'

'Blackmail, Kaitlin?'

'It isn't even as if you needed the money.'

'That's quite a statement,' Flynn drawled.

'If you really needed money, you wouldn't be content to accept my services. You'd insist on a cheque. Why are you doing this to me, Flynn?'

'I have my reasons, Kaitlin.'

'Don't tell me my services are so valuable to you.'

'Would I be asking you to perform them if they weren't?' A small pause. Then Flynn said, 'Will you come to the banquet, Kaitlin?'

If she didn't love him so desperately, Kaitlin would not think twice about going to the banquet. An evening in Flynn's company, and another payment taken care of. What could be easier? Yet as it was, loving Flynn as she did, the idea of filling in for another woman was unbelievably painful.

'If I refuse?' she whispered over dry lips.

'I don't have to spell out the answer for you, Kaitlin.'

'You'd really foreclose? You'd take my ranch?' Her legs were so weak, she felt they would buckle beneath her. 'Don't you have any heart, Flynn?' To Kaitlin's horror, the last words came out on a sob.

A long silence followed the question. Had she finally, Kaitlin wondered, got through to Flynn?

'Tell you what,' he said at last, 'why don't you think about it? You have until tomorrow to give me your answer.'

In the end, of course, there wasn't much to think about. Flynn didn't sound unduly surprised when he phoned, and Kaitlin told him her decision.

'I'll hate every moment,' she said tersely.

Flynn laughed. 'You're not going to an execution, Kaitlin. You might even enjoy yourself.'

Kaitlin closed her eyes. If only Flynn had invited her to be his date from the start. As it was...

'I won't enjoy it.' Her voice was strangled. 'I don't even have anything to wear to the banquet.'

'You surprise me,' he said drily.

Kaitlin swallowed over the bad taste in her mouth. 'You can't be thinking of the green gown.'

'Of course.'

'It was never meant for me, Flynn.'

'It's there for you now.'

'Another woman's gown.'

'A dream of a gown, Kaitlin.'

'Bought for someone else, I can't see myself wearing it.'

'While I can picture you in it.' Flynn's voice was huskily soft, infinitely seductive. 'A sexy vision in green. There won't be a man who won't long to dance with you, Kaitlin. They'll wish they could hold you in their arms. They'll all be envying me, every one of those wealthy oilmen. They'll imagine me kissing you—'

Kaitlin felt the blood heating in her veins. Feverishly, she pushed a hand through dishevelled hair, glad that Flynn couldn't see her doing it. 'Don't,' she said, a little desperately.

'They'll imagine me making love to you—'

'*Don't*!'

'They'll picture you in my bed.'

'You don't know when to stop!' Kaitlin shouted furiously.

'Can't you picture it, Kaitlin?'

His voice, soft and evocative, was sending shivers through her body. 'No,' she said weakly.

'Kaitlin… Kaitlin, try.'

'I don't think it's a good idea, after all. The banquet, the dress. It's all a big mistake.' From somewhere she summoned the strength to speak. 'I must have been crazy to agree to go with you.'

'What are you saying, Kaitlin?' The seductiveness had left his tone.

'I won't go to the banquet, Flynn.'

'You've changed your mind?'

'That's right.'

If she expected an argument she didn't get it. 'If that's what you want,' was all he said.

'Flynn… Will you give me some extra time to make my next payment?'

He sounded amused. 'You know better than to ask me that.'

'It's the banquet or foreclosure? Don't you care that I'm desperate? Can't you show some compassion?'

'Not the kind of compassion you seem to want.'

Kaitlin was silent. If there was anything she could say to win Flynn over, she did not know what it was.

'I'll say goodbye now,' Flynn said. 'I have a meeting to go to, and I'm starting to run late. So I guess we'll just forget the banquet?'

In that moment Kaitlin understood that pride and her love for Flynn were about to lose her the ranch.

Over a painful throat, she said, 'Flynn, wait!'

'Kaitlin?'

'I… I'll go to the banquet.' Each word she spoke came out with effort.

'You've changed your mind again?'

'…Yes.'

'Great,' was all he said.

To Kaitlin's chagrin, Flynn seemed to be taking her change of heart very much in his stride. She leaned against the wall and closed her eyes as he went on talking. 'I'll pick you up on Saturday morning, Kaitlin. The business part of the convention will be over by then.'

'Fine.'

And don't worry about the dress, I'll bring it with me when I come.'

'Flynn,' she said, as he seemed about to put down the phone, 'I want you to be certain about one thing.'

'What is that, Kaitlin?'

'I've agreed to go to the banquet with you—but only because I don't seem to have any choice.'

CHAPTER EIGHT

FLYNN knocked at the door on the stroke of seven. Kaitlin took a calming breath and a last look in the mirror. Would he guess, she wondered as she went to meet him, how many hours she had spent debating with herself in the hotel room?

Which dress should she wear to the banquet? She had two choices. There was the old pink dress, which Flynn did not know about, worn to different parties in an era when parties had been a part of Kaitlin's world. And the green gown, inspiration of a designer with magical hands.

The pink dress was pretty, the green gown was bewitching. The pink dress was made for a young girl on the threshold of adult life. The green gown was made for a woman in love.

The pink dress had been bought for Kaitlin by parents who adored her. The green gown had been bought for another woman, by a man who would never love Kaitlin.

The other woman... A woman without a name. *She* should have been with Flynn tonight. What had happened to change that particular arrangement? And how disappointed was Flynn? He must care very much about the woman to have wanted to buy her something so costly and exquisite.

Laying the two dresses side by side on the bed, Kaitlin had wavered between one and the another, deciding at last on the pink dress. With an hour to spare before the start of the banquet, she had showered and dressed—and looked in the mirror.

'I look nice,' she'd said to herself. 'Nice—and ordinary.'

Her eyes went to the bed on which still lay the green gown. Her fingers reached towards it, touched the soft fabric, drew back abruptly, touched again. Temptation racked

her. There was a part of Kaitlin that wanted, more than
anything, to wear the gown. For herself. *And for Flynn*.
She loved Flynn, and she yearned to be beautiful in his
eyes—even if he was in love with someone else.

The second decision was made in an instant. A decision
that was made with the heart rather than the mind.

She moved quickly now. It was a matter of a few minutes
to take off the one dress, and replace it with the other.
When that was done, she sat down in front of the mirror
and put on a little more make-up: a dusting of green eyeshadow, mascara, a different shade of lipstick.

Flynn's knock came just as she was hanging the pink
dress back in the closet.

'Well…' he said when Kaitlin opened the door.

It was all he said for at least a minute. He just stood
there looking down at her. In his eyes was an expression
Kaitlin had never seen before. A look of naked desire.
Kaitlin's breath jerked in her throat.

'Say something,' she whispered at last.

'The cowgirl—transformed into an alluring woman.'
Flynn's voice, deep and rough, sent shivers through Kaitlin.

Unable to hold his gaze, she turned away, only to feel
his hand on her arm. 'Let me look at you, Kaitlin.'

Beneath the intensity of the very male gaze, she felt more
tremulous than ever. 'Shouldn't we… Shouldn't we be going?'

'In a moment. Kaitlin, you look…'

'What?' she asked unsteadily.

'Even more beautiful than the day in the store.'

Kaitlin had never been happier. At that moment it didn't
seem important that she wasn't the woman Flynn had meant
to spend this evening with. All that mattered was that he
was looking at her with the eyes of a lover.

When he said, 'Close your eyes,' she didn't argue, but
did as he asked, gasping when she felt something slide
around her throat, cold as ice against her warm skin.
Flynn's hands moved at the back of her neck, before going
to her shoulders.

'You can look now,' he said softly, when he had turned
her around.

Opening her eyes, Kaitlin found herself staring into the mirror, Flynn close behind her, just as they had stood together in the fitting-room of the boutique. For a long moment all she could see was their two heads, the one many inches below the other. Wider than she was, extending beyond her on both sides, was a pair of male shoulders, encased in the jacket of a grey tuxedo.

And then she saw the necklace around her throat.

'Flynn! This is… It's incredible!'

'It's supposed to go with the dress.'

'It's gorgeous! That huge green stone—is it an emerald? It sets off the colour of the dress.'

'As well as your eyes.'

'Yes…' she agreed after a moment. 'Flynn, I'm astounded, I wouldn't have thought you knew a thing about jewellery.'

'A cowboy like me—at home on his horse, with a lariat in one hand and the reins in the other.' His eyes gleamed with mischief.

She threw him an answering smile in the mirror. 'Something like that.'

'Want the truth, Kaitlin?'

'Yes.'

'I don't know about jewellery,' he admitted. 'I told the girl in the store about the dress, and she helped me choose this necklace.'

For a little while Kaitlin had actually forgotten the other woman's existence, but now she remembered. 'Just as I helped you choose the dress,' she said quietly.

'A man needs help with some things.'

He seemed not to have noticed her change of tone. 'I can't wear this,' she said.

'Why not?'

'It wasn't meant for me.'

In the mirror, Flynn's expression was enigmatic. 'You agreed to wear the dress.'

'…Yes.'

'Why not the necklace?'

'It's more personal.'

'You could tell yourself,' Flynn suggested, 'that the necklace was meant to be worn with the dress.'

'But not by me.'

'By the person wearing the dress.'

A person who was someone other than Kaitlin. Reluctantly, her hands lifted to open the clasp of the necklace.

'Keep it on,' Flynn said softly, his tone so seductive that Kaitlin had to lower her eyelids, lest he glimpse the effect he was having on her. Her breathing grew shallow as his hands lifted from her shoulders, up to her hands, covering them, caressing her throat with his fingers. In a matter of seconds he had succeeded in sending the familiar burning sensations coursing through her.

'Wear it for me,' he said, his lips touching her hair.

'You don't understand—' her voice shook '—how difficult it is for me to wear something that wasn't intended for me.'

'There's no one but you and me here now, Kaitlin.'

With the dark eyes holding hers in the mirror, and the long fingers creating fire on her throat, it was getting harder and harder to think. Nevertheless she managed to say, 'That isn't the point, Flynn.'

'There's just one point, Kaitlin—I want you to wear the necklace.' His fingers moved slowly over her fevered skin. 'Will you?'

Her mind told her she should refuse him, her heart forbade her to say the words. Once more, Kaitlin understood that she could not deny him.

'The most beautiful woman in the place tonight.'

It was long past midnight. The banquet was over, and they were standing in the doorway of Kaitlin's hotel room. Two rooms, that had been the condition on which she had insisted, and Flynn had not objected. His own room was down the hall.

'Not a man who wasn't wishing you were in his arms tonight, Kaitlin.'

'Aren't you exaggerating, Flynn?'

Though she hadn't consumed more than two or three

glasses of wine all evening, Kaitlin felt a little drunk: drunk on fun and laughter; drunk on the admiration of the men Flynn had introduced her to, a few of whom had made passes which she had ignored; drunk, more than anything else, on the happiness of being in Flynn's arms on the dance-floor, being held close to the long hard body, feeling the erotic movements of hard legs against hers.

'Not *every* man, surely?' she teased.

'Without exception,' he teased back.

'You didn't fare too badly, either, Flynn—there were several women who were devouring you with their eyes.'

'Were there?'

'I thought you might leave me stranded while you went off and made love to one of them.'

'There was only one woman with whom I wanted to do that—and I wanted it very badly.' His eyes were deep and very dark.

'Who was she?' Kaitlin asked over the rapid beating of her heart.

'Don't you know?'

'How can I, when you haven't told me her name?'

'She's standing just inches from me.'

'Flynn…' Kaitlin said over lips that were suddenly dry.

'I still want to make love to her.'

'It… It's very late.'

'Is it?'

'Yes.' She pretended to look at her watch. 'We're both tired, and—'

'I've never felt more awake in my life—in more ways than one, Kaitlin.'

'I think you should go, Flynn. It's time for us both to get to bed.'

'You're right, it is time for bed. Together, Kaitlin, both of us together in one bed.'

She opened her mouth to say something, but he put a finger over her lips. 'I've been wanting to make love to you all evening,' he said raggedly. 'There wasn't a moment when I wasn't thinking of it. Kaitlin… Kaitlin, I believe you wanted it, too.'

It was true, of course. Through all the fun of the banquet

and the dance that had followed, Kaitlin had been aware of
Flynn constantly, hungering for his kisses, yearning for the
fulfillment that only this one man would ever be able to
give her.

She did not stop him as he closed the door of her room.
When he put out his arms to her, she went to him willingly.
Her whole body was on fire as he drew her to him. For a
long moment they clung together, barely moving as they
savoured an exquisite closeness. Kaitlin's heart was beating
so hard that she was certain that Flynn must be able to feel
it and hear it; she fancied that she could feel his heart
against her throat.

He began to kiss her: soft kisses at first, a butterfly touching of lips, incredibly tender, and for some reason extremely erotic. But the kisses did not stay tender for long.
They became deep, passionate, with Flynn calling for a
response from Kaitlin, and receiving it. For a while they
kissed as if they could not get enough of each other. And
all the time they were caressing, exploring, relearning the
shape and feel of each other.

Once Flynn lifted his head. 'Do you feel it too, Kaitlin?'

Through dazed eyes she looked up at him. 'Feel what?'

'The years slipping away. As if the time apart never ex-
isted?'

'Yes…'

'As if we need to make up for all the kissing we've
missed.'

'Yes!'

The breath hissed in his throat as he pulled her even
closer, his cowboy arms hard as steel around her slender
body, his hands sliding over her back, her throat, over her
breasts and hips beneath the green dress. His kisses were
even deeper now, his tongue exploring the sweetness of her
mouth. And Kaitlin, driven by her own fierce need, kissed
him back with all the hungry abandon that was in her, holding nothing back. Beneath his lips, she let out small cries
of pleasure, and heard him groan.

'Kaitlin,' he said, tearing his lips from her mouth. 'Sexy,
lovely Kaitlin. There'll be no stopping tonight.'

'I know that,' she whispered. 'I… I want it, too, Flynn.'

Another groan rose from deep in his throat. Kaitlin was awed, overcome with the knowledge that she could affect this tough man so intensely.

Tenderly, he began to undress her, and all the while she could feel his passion just beneath the surface. Off came the dress, but he insisted on leaving on the necklace. When she was naked, he took a step backwards.

'Let me look at you, Kaitlin.'

She stood still, a little shy beneath his gaze, yet exulting in the expression she saw in his eyes. God, but she loved this man!

'You are so beautiful,' he said huskily. 'I remember a girl, but you've become a woman, Kaitlin. A gorgeous, sexy, desirable woman.'

And then he was closing the distance between them, and saying, 'Undress me, too, sweet.'

Sweet... The endearment which he had used so long ago made her heart race.

Shyly, and yet eagerly, she did as he asked, only fumbling a little at the end, when she removed his underwear. He told her that she didn't have to worry, that he would protect her. She nodded, and didn't tell him how much it would mean to her to have his child, even if they were not married. At least that way there would always be a part of him in her life.

There was no time to talk anyway, as he lifted her in his arms and carried her to the bed.

For a long time they lay there, welded together, mouth to mouth, arms and legs entwined. Then Flynn found Kaitlin's breasts, caressing each breast in turn, first with his hands and then with his lips, turning up the fire in Kaitlin's loins. She was caressing him, too, exploring him, delighting in shaping her hands over the hard male muscles of his chest and shoulders and arms.

Their lovemaking was everything she had dreamed it could be; sensation, passion, excitement. And at last, when Flynn entered her, minutes upon minute of sheer blinding ecstasy, the world consisting of only two people and of the wonder they were creating together.

For a while afterwards they lay still, wrapped in each

other's arms. Flynn was so quiet that Kaitlin was certain he was sleeping. She was startled when he spoke.

'Why didn't you tell me?'

'Tell you what?' she murmured.

'That you were a virgin.'

'Oh…' She tensed.

'Why didn't you say something, Kaitlin?'

'I never thought… Does it matter?'

'Matter?' His voice was so odd, the tone one she had never heard before. 'Yes, Kaitlin, it matters.'

The tone, as much as the words, made Kaitlin tense. Memories flooded back of the day five years earlier when Flynn had pleaded with her to make love with him. 'After my party,' she could still hear herself saying the words. But the morning after he'd washed her back, and without a word to her, Flynn had gone off on the cattle drive. She had seen him only once more, after her party, in a bar with another woman in his arms.

To this day Kaitlin wondered if he had found her inadequate, and looked for a means to get away from her. Did he find her inadequate again now?

Numbly, she said, 'You didn't enjoy it.'

'It was fantastic! Wasn't it good for you, Kaitlin?'

'More than that. But, Flynn, why does it matter that I was a virgin?'

'I thought… I was certain there'd been other men.'

Other men, when all these years, in some part of her mind, there had been only Flynn?

'Nobody who mattered enough,' Kaitlin said.

Again she heard Flynn groan. Then he was drawing her to him again, covering her with kisses, her mouth and throat and breasts, raising her once more to the heights.

They slept after that, tired, spent, still wrapped in each other's arms.

'Hi, there, gorgeous.'

The first light of dawn was seeping into the room when Kaitlin awoke to see the most wonderful sight in all the world—Flynn's face beside hers on the pillow.

She smiled at him through sleepy eyes. 'Hi, yourself.'

'How do you feel, Kaitlin?'

'Wonderful.'

'That's good, because I feel wonderful, too. We had quite a night, didn't we?'

'Quite a night,' she agreed with a smile.

'We can have a great day too.'

'What do you have in mind, cowboy?'

'Should I tell you, Kaitlin? Or should I show you? Actually, I think showing is more fun.'

Flynn began to kiss her, and she kissed him, too, with all the love that was in her. When his mouth left hers, and went to her breasts, she buried her hands in the glossy hair at the back of his head. Only a few hours had gone by since their last lovemaking, yet already the familiar sensations of excitement and desire were beginning to stir.

She was kissing his shoulders when Flynn lifted his head and looked down at her. 'In case you're still wondering— this was what I had in mind.'

Kaitlin laughed softly. 'I gathered.'

'I think we should spend all day making love.'

'Do you never get tired, Flynn?'

'Tired? With you in my arms? Never.'

Wonderful words, Kaitlin felt as if she could never get enough of them.

'We'll have some breakfast, then make love all morning,' he said. 'We'll go out for a snack, then come right back to this room and go on where we left off. What do you say, Kaitlin?'

She was about to tell him that the suggestion was fantastic, and right in line with her own wishes, when, as if out of nowhere, reality struck.

'Flynn, the ranch.'

'What about it?'

'I should be getting back.'

He laughed against her lips. 'What's your hurry?'

'I have work to do.'

'Nonsense.'

'Don't tell me you've forgotten?'

'I haven't forgotten a thing. Not a single thing, Kaitlin.'

In an entirely different tone, he added, 'Actually, you won't have to work so hard any more. Maybe you won't have to work at all.'

She stared at him. 'What do you mean, Flynn?'

'What I said.'

'Why?' she asked after a moment. 'Why won't I have to work so hard? Has something changed since last night?'

Propping himself on one elbow, Flynn looked down at her. 'You don't know the answer?'

One answer came to mind. An answer that was so thoroughly repellent that her blood ran cold. No, Kaitlin thought, not that. Please, Flynn, never that.

'I do need an answer,' she said carefully. 'Why won't I have to work so hard any more?'

'Can't you guess, Kaitlin?'

Tensely, she said, 'You're letting me off another payment?'

Flynn's eyes, those wonderful dark eyes, were alive and sparkling as he grinned at her. 'I had a feeling you'd come up with the answer yourself.'

'That's it then?'

The sparkle intensified. 'Of course.'

'We made love, and you're letting me off a payment.'

'Not just one payment, Kaitlin. You see, sweet—'

'Got out of my room, Flynn,' she interrupted him.

'Now?' he asked disbelievingly. 'I'm in the middle of telling you something.'

She felt sick. 'I don't want to hear it. Go, Flynn.'

'This is silly.'

'Get out of my bed,' she ordered, as steadily as she could. It was very difficult to talk calmly, when her mind was telling her one thing, and her body was clamouring for something quite different.

Flynn's voice changed. 'Kaitlin, what's come over you?'

'Please,' she said, over a dry throat, 'just get out of my bed.'

'Are you serious?' He was looking at her as if she had just turned into a stranger.

'Quite serious.'

'I don't understand you, we had a wonderful time last night.'

'We did,' she agreed unsteadily.

'Yet now you're kicking me out.'

'I'm *asking* you to leave.'

'I don't understand you, Kaitlin.' His voice was hard now.

'It's simple—last night was a mistake.'

'It wasn't a mistake, Kaitlin, not for either of us.'

He tried to reach for her, but she managed to pull away from him, rolling as far as she could to the other side of the bed.

'It was a mistake,' she insisted. 'Forget it happened.'

'You can't mean that, Kaitlin!'

'As much as I've ever meant anything. Are you going to get out of my bed, Flynn, or do I have to call security?'

He looked down at her a long moment, his expression grim. 'You won't need security,' he told her flatly.

Kaitlin lay very still, trying not to watch Flynn as he left her bed and roughly pulled on his clothes. He did not look back as he walked out of the door, and she did not call to him.

It was only when the door had closed behind Flynn, that Kaitlin's control left her. She began to shake, so violently that even her teeth clattered.

When the shaking began to abate, her eyes went to the beautiful green gown, still lying on the chair where Flynn had dropped it. The most beautiful dress in the world. How tenderly Flynn had taken it off her. And the necklace… She touched the big emerald that still nestled in the hollow of her throat.

With an exclamation of disgust, she ripped off the necklace and tossed it onto the gown, the two things that had never been intended for her in the first place. She turned her head, so that she would not have to look at them.

But it was impossible not to remember. Flynn was everywhere: behind her eyelids, imprinted on her mind, his body as warm and alive as if he was still lying beside her in the bed. There were the things he had said: she was the most beautiful woman in the world, their kisses would make up for all the years they had lost.

She had believed everything. Every word. Because she had *wanted* so badly to believe. How amused Flynn must have been by her ardour and her passion. Well, and why not? He had conned her into doing exactly what he wanted.

'You bought me, Flynn Henderson,' she said bitterly, into the silence of the empty room. 'I slept with you because I'm in love with you. Whereas for you it was services rendered. *Services—how I hate that word*! I gave you all the sex you wanted, in exchange for which you planned to let me off more payments. Why weren't you honest with me, Flynn? I'd have told you that I'm not a prostitute.'

Last night had been the most wonderful night of her life. Just hours later she felt cheap, exploited and abused.

'How could you, Flynn?' she asked on a sob.

Turning on her face, she wept into her pillow until there were no tears left.

CHAPTER NINE

THE FIRST thing Kaitlin did when she got back to the ranch, was to put a message on her answering machine. She sensed that Flynn would phone, and the last thing she wanted was to talk to him.

Phone he did. Every day for a while, several times a day occasionally. Kaitlin had no intention of returning his calls, and his messages, friendly at first, began to sound more and more impatient.

His last message was brusque to the point of anger. 'Dammit, Kaitlin, this is becoming ridiculous! If you think I'll keep trying your number, you're mistaken.'

Kaitlin told herself it was a relief to have no contact with Flynn—and tried not to admit to herself how much she was missing him. It was true that she loved him deeply, equally true that her feelings would never be reciprocated. Flynn made no secret of the fact that he was attracted to her, but Kaitlin knew the attraction was purely physical, love did not come into it. And that could never be enough for her.

Besides, there was the other woman. The mysterious woman whom Flynn cared for so much that he had bought her an expensive dress and an even more expensive piece of jewellery. Was he still seeing her? How deep was their attachment? All questions which Kaitlin agonized over, questions which she would not lower herself to ask Flynn.

The weeks passed. By day, Kaitlin was working as hard as ever, and so were the ranch cowboys. In the evenings she sat with her accounts and ledgers spread around her on the kitchen table. She was beginning—just—to make ends meet. There were even times when she let herself hope that financially things would turn out all right.

And then she would remember the mortgage payments. True to his word, Flynn had let a few weeks go by without asking for payment. But the respite—one that he evidently felt she had earned when she'd allowed him to make love to her—would end any day.

He phoned late one evening, when Kaitlin was already half asleep, and she answered the call without thinking.

'I guess you weren't expecting me.' He sounded amused.

Instantly awake, Kaitlin tensed at the sound of his voice: the beautiful voice, low and vibrant, and so attractive that in seconds her body throbbed with longing.

'I should have expected you,' she said numbly, 'but I didn't.'

'Lucky for me, because otherwise I would have got your answering machine again. Why do you never return my calls, Kaitlin?'

'I've been busy.'

'Too busy to spend a few minutes on the phone?'

'What do you think, Flynn?'

'Obviously, you don't want to talk to me.'

'Brilliant deduction,' she said caustically.

'Just as you refused to talk when I flew you back to the ranch the day after the banquet. What happened, Kaitlin? Why did you turn so cold right after we'd made love?'

Kaitlin felt a hard knot of tension forming in her stomach. 'Goodbye, Flynn,' she whispered.

'*Not so fast*! I need to know what happened. One moment you were ardent and passionate, the next, you were icy and hostile. Why, Kaitlin?'

'I don't want to talk about it,' she said unsteadily.

'I have to know.'

'But I can't give you an answer. So if there's nothing else, I'm going to hang up now.'

'There is something, Kaitlin.'

After a moment, she said slowly, 'It's that time again.'

'Not quite yet—remember, after the banquet I let you off an additional payment?'

'I remember.' Her voice was flat. 'Even so, it will be payment time soon.'

A short silence. Then, in an entirely new voice, Flynn said, 'You won't need any money, Kaitlin.'

'Why am I not surprised? I guess you have another service in mind for me, Flynn?'

If he registered the sarcasm, he did not comment on it. 'I want you to pack a suitcase, Kaitlin.'

In a second all her senses were alert. 'A suitcase?'

'That's right.'

'Filled with what exactly, Flynn?'

'Clothes. Enough for two weeks.'

'Two weeks!' Every nerve was jangling.

'For a start. We can take care of the rest later. Not that you'll be wearing very much.'

Kaitlin gripped the phone so tightly that her knuckles were white. 'You have some nerve, Flynn.'

'Do I, Kaitlin?'

'You know you do,' she said brittly. 'Two weeks, Flynn—where?'

The laughter that came to her through the telephone line was so seductive that she felt dizzy. 'That,' he said 'is a surprise.'

What on earth had he dreamed up for her this time? It appalled Kaitlin how much she wanted to know the answer. It was a moment before she remembered that no matter how deeply she felt about Flynn, his own plans for her were always propelled by some motive. In this particular case, the motive was not difficult to guess.

'I can't leave the ranch for two weeks, Flynn.'

'Sure, you can,' came the cheerful retort.

'No,' Kaitlin said firmly. 'Two days were bad enough. Two weeks are impossible. I don't know what service you have in mind—judging by the things you've said I don't think I want to know—but it doesn't really matter because my answer won't change.'

'If you don't think you have enough cowboys to keep the ranch going in your absence, I'll help you work things out.'

'I've never needed your help, Flynn.'

He laughed. 'Independent Kaitlin, always so feisty. Has it occurred to you, sweet, that you might enjoy what I have planned?'

Sweet...

'Don't call me that, Flynn,' she said grimly. 'And just tell me one thing—would the two weeks away involve sleeping with you?'

The voice that came through the line to her was vital and intoxicatingly sexy. 'That's part of it.'

Two weeks of lovemaking. Waking in the morning and finding Flynn in bed next to her. The idea was sheer bliss. *But she could not give in to him.* 'The answer is no, Flynn.'

'Actually,' he said, as if he hadn't heard her, 'two weeks would just be the start.'

Anger was beginning to stir inside her, a deep and intense anger. How dare Flynn treat her as if she was some cheap woman, always available for his physical needs?

'Exactly how long do you have in mind?' she asked acidly.

'A long time, Kaitlin. Very long.'

'Long as in how long, Flynn? Weeks?'

'Longer than that.'

He had a nerve! An absolute and utter nerve. She would tell him so in no uncertain terms. But not before she knew a few more facts. And that meant playing along with him.

Carefully, keeping her voice as calm as she could make it, she said, 'What would be in this for me, Flynn?'

Silence followed the question. A strange silence.

'What would be in it for me?' Kaitlin asked again.

'What do you think?' His tone was odd.

'Judging by the past, I assume you're going to let me off more payments.'

'There would be no more payments.'

'None at all?' she asked disbelievingly.

'You heard me.'

Kaitlin closed her eyes. No more payments. No more worries about the ranch. To be unencumbered, free. To live without the constant worry of how to prevent her beloved home from being taken away from her.

And yet she would not be free at all. For there would always be Flynn, and the demands he would make of her. Demands that would be a joy if they were made in love.

But there was no love on Flynn's part, and that made any arrangement unacceptable.

'What you're proposing,' Kaitlin said, 'is that I become your mistress.'

'I don't remember using the word.'

'What other word is there?'

'How about wife?' he asked softly.

'*Wife*!' She felt the blood drain from her cheeks.

'I'm asking you to marry me, Kaitlin.'

When she could speak, she said, 'This isn't the first time you've asked me.'

'That's right.'

She remembered the last time Flynn had proposed marriage, and she thought of his grand plan. He would own the ranch, no matter what it took. And he wanted Kaitlin as well. After all these years, his ambition was about to become reality. Or so he thought.

'The answer is still no,' she said.

'You haven't given it any thought.' That odd tone again.

'I don't have to.'

'Think of it, Kaitlin. No more payments, and you'd still have your ranch.'

'And I'd have to spend every night in your bed.'

'I could have sworn you enjoyed it the last time we were together. Don't tell me you're just a good actress, Kaitlin?'

'One night,' she managed to whisper. 'We had a good time at the banquet. And I... Well, one thing led to another, didn't it? But I've had time to think since then. I wish it hadn't happened.'

'Is that why you've been refusing to answer my calls?'

'...Yes.'

After a long moment, Flynn said, 'Why don't you think about my proposal, Kaitlin?'

'There's nothing to think about, Flynn. I wouldn't have come to you as a mistress—and I won't come to you as a wife either.'

'If that's the case, why did you want to know what was in it for you?'

'Curiosity. I was just interested in knowing what you'd

offer. The fact is, Flynn, I don't have to think about your proposal, because the answer will never change.'

His voice very hard suddenly, Flynn said, 'I see.'

'I hope you do. You need to understand, I'd rather risk losing my ranch than marry you.'

A long silence followed her last words.

At last, Kaitlin said, 'About the payments...'

'What about them?'

'I'll find a way of making them.'

Her voice was as firm as she could make it. She had to hope that it hid her doubts and fears.

'Faster, Star! Faster! There's a horse. Oh, there's a good horse.'

Lithely the gelding responded to Kaitlin's commands, weaving around the three barrels that she had placed at strategic intervals along the corral. This way and that Star raced, in and around and out, perilously close to the barrels sometimes, yet never so close as to knock them down.

Another round completed. Reining in the gelding, Kaitlin glanced at her watch and saw that she had broken her own record. She was riding fast and well, she thought elatedly. Her rapport with her horse was fantastic, and her speed and skill were improving every day. If only she could find a way of shaving another five seconds off her riding time. She would do it, she vowed. But she must do it soon, for the rodeo was just ten days away.

After her last phone call with Flynn, Kaitlin had spent a sleepless night. 'Marry me,' he had said, not for the first time since he had come back to the ranch, tempting her with the one thing she wanted more than anything else. A life with Flynn. But at what cost! Marriage to a man she loved more deeply than she had ever imagined herself loving a man. Marriage to a man who would never have anything but contempt for the woman who had allowed herself to be bought.

Not for a second did she regret her answer.

And yet there was still the matter of the mortgage. What would Flynn do now that she had turned down his offer?

Take over the ranch? Not if she could help it! But what could she do to bring in some money?

The answer came to her suddenly. *Rodeo*! She remembered thinking about it for a few moments in the restaurant in Austin, when Flynn had told her about his days on the circuit. Why had she never thought of it since then? Flynn had made money on the circuit. What he could do, she could do, too. She jerked up in bed, her body rigid with excitement.

Of the events in which women participated, barrel-racing appealed to Kaitlin most, and it was popular with the crowds. Briefly she thought of the cowgirls already working the circuit, all of them more experienced than she was. She could not let that thought intimidate her, she decided. She was an excellent horsewoman, and as far as riding went she had as much experience as the next person. She had to believe it was possible for her to win. What she needed now was practice.

Once more around the corral, she decided. Then she would give Star a well-earned rest.

Off she rode, zig-zagging her way from one barrel to the next, with fleet-footed Star responding to her slightest command. A minute later, the stopwatch revealed another good round.

Kaitlin was walking the horse back to the stable, when a tall figure emerged from the pines beyond the corral.

'Flynn!'

'Hi, Kaitlin,' he drawled.

'How long have you been here?'

'Long enough.'

His tone was so accusing that her chin lifted. 'What's that supposed to mean?'

'I've been here long enough to wonder what's going on.'

'I beg your pardon?' she countered hotly. 'This is still my ranch, Flynn, and whatever I do here is my business only.'

In a second, he had vaulted the fence, and taken hold of Star's rein. 'What are you up to, Kaitlin?'

Her heart began to beat uncomfortably fast: Flynn was

many things, but he had never been stupid. Lightly she said, 'Just having a bit of fun with the barrels.'

'Fun?' He tossed the word at her tersely.

She shrugged. 'A bit of sport.'

'A rodeo sport, Kaitlin.'

'Now that you say so.'

'Which you just happen to be indulging in for your entertainment.'

'Why not?'

His hand snaked out and caught her chin, his fingers biting into the soft skin. Alert though she was to the danger he presented, Kaitlin could not help being excited. It was so long since she had seen Flynn.

'I hope you're not thinking of taking part in a rodeo, Kaitlin.'

'Would you care, Flynn?'

The eyes that raked her face were unsmiling, and his expression was ominous. 'We talked about this once before,' he told her flatly. 'I warned you that rodeo-riding can be dangerous. You could get hurt, Kaitlin.'

'I say now what I said then—if I did get hurt, that shouldn't bother you.'

'It does,' he said flatly.

'Why?' She threw the question at him cheekily. 'Why would *you* care if *I* got hurt? It would make life much simpler for you if I wasn't around.'

His eyelids came down over his eyes, so that she could not see the expression in them. 'I'd care about any woman who got hurt,' he told her.

Before she could let the pain of the impersonal answer get to her, he added, 'Bottom line, Kaitlin, you are not entering a rodeo.'

'Bottom line to *you*, Flynn—you couldn't stop me if I did.'

The pressure of the fingers on her chin hardened. 'Couldn't I?'

She threw him a look filled with challenge. 'No, Flynn you could not.'

He muttered an oath. Clearly, he was growing impatient. '*Are* you going to take part in a rodeo, Kaitlin?'

He was too close to her. After the weeks apart, his touch, unloverlike though it was, was alarmingly arousing. Still, Kaitlin knew that she must force herself to concentrate on the matter in hand.

Pulling her chin out of his hand, she said firmly, 'I don't have to answer you, Flynn.' Where his fingers had been, the skin felt cold.

The tall cowboy was persistent. 'Is this your way of getting money for your mortgage payments, Kaitlin? If it is, I forbid you to try it.'

'Forbid, Flynn?' Her voice threw out a dare to him.

'You heard me. Say so, if you need an extension.'

'You haven't agreed to one up till now.'

'There's always a first time.'

Tempting words, but Kaitlin decided it wasn't a good idea to accept favours from Flynn.

Eyes sparkling, she said, 'I don't need an extension.'

Something moved in his face. 'I see. Care to tell me how you'll raise the money?'

'I don't care to.'

'I need your assurance that you won't take part in a rodeo.'

'I can't give you that. And I still don't know why it means so much to you.'

'I've already given you a reason.'

'Other women ride in rodeos.'

'Cowgirls with experience. You've never ridden in a rodeo in your life.'

'It would be a first for me in that case.'

'Kaitlin,' he growled impatiently.

She flashed him a cheeky grin. 'Come on, Flynn, don't you think you're making a big deal out of nothing? You're assuming that I'm going to be entering a rodeo, I haven't said that I am.'

'If you were, you wouldn't tell me.'

'True,' she said. 'By the way, Flynn, you haven't told me why you're here. According to my calculations, the next payment isn't due today.'

'I wanted to talk to you about that.'

'We've talked already.'

'Face to face, Kaitlin.'

'Goodness, Flynn, how intriguing. I expect you've come up with another fascinating offer.'

His eyes took on a sudden gleam. 'The same one actually.'

Inside Kaitlin, emotions were raging. She wanted nothing more than to go into Flynn's arms. A treacherous voice questioned if it would really be so bad to accept his marriage proposal—even if he did not love her.

She gave herself a firm mental shake. How could she let herself think this way, even for a second? Obviously, she must get rid of him quickly, while she still had her sanity.

'Don't you realize you're wasting your time?' From somewhere she summoned the strength to make her voice hard. 'You can make the offer as tempting as you like, but nothing you can say will change my mind.'

'Nothing, Kaitlin?' His gaze was searching.

'You heard me.'

'Nothing at all?'

As firmly as she could, Kaitlin said, 'Nothing. Not a thing you could say would change my mind. I meant what I said on the phone, Flynn—I won't give in to you, even if it means losing my ranch.'

On Star's back, a nervous Kaitlin willed herself to relax. The arena was a mass of sound and smells and activity. Music blared, announcers shouted through amplifiers. The air was heavy with the smell of sawdust and hay.

People in Stetsons and tight-fitting jeans were everywhere.

These were the seasoned people of the circuit: cowboys who travelled from one rodeo to another, riding bulls and bronco horses, proudly wearing scars that spoke of falls and other injuries, sporting belt buckles denoting the competitions they had won; cowgirls who rode broncos, too, or penned cattle or barrel-raced. Attractive people, all of them, lithe and fit, tough and sure of themselves. People who knew each other from the circuit, who were friends despite their rivalry in the arena.

From the moment she had arrived at the rodeo, Kaitlin had been gripped by the excitement pervading the scene. It was an excitement that stayed with her as she unloaded Star from the boxcar, as she filled in her application and proudly rode with the other participants in the rodeo parade.

One event followed another: bronco-riding, cattle-penning and calf-roping. The crowd was large and enthusiastic, generously applauding both losers and winners.

At last the barrel-racers had their turn. One after another the cowgirls rode into the arena, racing their horses between the barrels, some executing the ride perfectly, others coming to grief when a barrel was knocked down. Kaitlin had drawn the last spot in the competition, and as she watched her rivals, her nervousness grew.

In the arena now, the second-last competitor raced her horse between the barrels. So far this girl was the best yet.

As she waited her turn on Star's back, Kaitlin wondered if she had been quite crazy to think of competing against so many experienced riders. Could she do half as well? Should she withdraw even now?

And then she remembered that the fate of her ranch depended on the outcome of this race. *She must do better than the others*.

The cowgirl left the arena to a roar of applause. The announcer called Kaitlin's name. Her nerves tightened almost to breaking-point.

She was about to give Star the command to start when a familiar voice shouted, '*Kaitlin*!'

Distracted, she looked aside. Flynn was vaulting the fence of the waiting area. 'Get off that horse!' he yelled.

'*No*!'

'Kaitlin Mullins,' boomed the announcer.

Flynn had a hand on Star's reins now. 'Turn the horse around!' he ordered.

'No! Let go, Flynn!'

Other voices now. Two security men had rushed to the scene. They were tugging at Flynn's arms, demanding to know how he had got into the private waiting area.

'Kaitlin Mullins,' boomed the announcer again.

'Arrest the guy,' shouted a security man.

'Don't be a fool, man.' This from Flynn, as he jerked himself easily free of the man. 'You know me, Jim.'

'What the hell…' The security man stopped in mid-sentence. His face changed. '*Flynn! Flynn Henderson!* Good God, man, what are you doing here?'

'What I have to. Let go of me, Jim! You, too, Mel.'

'How did you get in here?'

'Wasn't difficult.'

Flynn threw the men a grin, and as they grinned back at him, it came to Kaitlin that to the people of the rodeo world Flynn Henderson was a hero, a bull-rider of renown. He would have had little difficulty getting through doors and gates that were barred to lesser mortals.

'Kaitlin Mullins!' called the announcer, starting to sound impatient now. 'Kaitlin Mullins!'

'The lady's about to ride,' the security man named Jim said to Flynn.

'No, she isn't.'

'She's a competitor, Flynn.'

'She thought she was.'

'Arrest him!' Kaitlin shouted.

'Take no notice,' Flynn advised. 'Sorry, guys, the lady and I are friends. I don't want her riding in any rodeo, and well she knows it.'

'Last call for Kaitlin Mullins!'

Kaitlin knew that if she did not make her appearance immediately she would be disqualified. Flynn was still talking to the security men, trying to convince them that she had no place in the arena, when Kaitlin spurred Star into action, knocking Flynn to his feet as she did so. Letting out an epithet Kaitlin had never heard him use before, he leaped up—too late to stop horse and rider.

Kaitlin rode into the arena, nerves tingling, heart beating wildly, body pumped with the additional adrenalin produced by the altercation with Flynn. *How dare he try to stop her from competing?*

As the first barrel came into view, she forced herself to concentrate. Briefly, panic rose inside her, but she managed to quell it. So much depended on this competition. She had to ride for her parents, her grandparents, for her home. She had to ride for herself, for her pride and self-esteem, for an independence which would not allow her to give in to Flynn's outrageous demands. *She had to ride despite Flynn*.

Rounding the first barrel, she went on to the next. As if Star sensed Kaitlin's extra momentum, the horse rose to the occasion, performing like a seasoned racer, responding to her slightest command. Round the second barrel the gelding raced, and on to the third. The roars of the crowd filled Kaitlin's ears. The extra adrenalin pumped in her veins and her throat. She was riding as she had never ridden before, fearlessly, flawlessly, fast as the wind.

When she reached the end, she needed no stopwatch to tell her that she had far surpassed her best practice run. Even before she looked at the clock, the thunderous applause greeting her performance from every side of the arena told her that she had won.

Bursting with pride, elated with her achievement, she gracefully acknowledged the applause, the judges and the crowd, before riding out of the arena. Dismounting, she gave Star a long hug of appreciation and thanks. 'Star, darling Star, you came through for me,' she crooned to her horse.

People were congratulating her on her ride now, but she barely noticed them. Some distance away was the only person who mattered. He was glowering at her, his face tight with a terrible anger.

Kaitlin ran to him. 'Flynn! Oh, Flynn, I did it!'

'So I saw.' His voice was flat, his face expressionless.

'How did you know where to find me?'

'Wasn't difficult. I just kept my eyes on every rodeo list in the state.'

'You didn't want me to compete, Flynn.'

'Damn right, I didn't!'

'You were wrong.'

'You could have broken your silly neck.'

'But I didn't!'

'Beginner's luck,' he said coldly.

'You're probably right. I may never manage it again. But I did it this time! Can't you be glad for me, Flynn?'

He looked down at her wordlessly, his wonderful eyes

filled with a bleakness Kaitlin had never before seen. His lips were a hard line, and a muscle moved in his throat.

Some of the elation drained out of Kaitlin. 'I appreciate your concern...'

'No, you don't, Kaitlin. All you care about is your moment of glory.'

'No! It's never been that. Never! I had to go through with it, don't you understand?'

'I understand,' Flynn said harshly.

'If you understand, why are you so angry?'

'If you don't know, there's no point telling you.'

Without another word, Flynn strode away, leaving Kaitlin to stare after him.

CHAPTER TEN

KAITLIN was out on the range when a small plane flew overhead. Gladly, she exclaimed, '*Flynn*!'

Less than twenty-four hours had passed since her triumph at the rodeo, a bitter-sweet triumph in the light of Flynn's reaction. The fact that he was coming to see her so soon must mean that his anger had cooled.

Eagerly she rode towards the airstrip, reaching it as the plane landed. Tethering her horse to a nearby post—not Star today, her darling Star deserved a good rest and lots of tender coddling—she ran on to the airstrip just as the tall figure was descending from his plane.

'Flynn!'

He could have met her halfway, but he didn't. Instead, he just stood watching her as she came to him.

'Hello, Kaitlin,' he said coolly.

Her happiness left her as she looked into the rugged face of the man she loved, hauteur and displeasure etched in every hard line and angle. Flynn's shoulders had a rigid squareness, his hands were shoved deep into his pockets.

Kaitlin took a step backwards. 'Flynn, what's wrong?' And when he didn't answer, 'You're still angry...'

He gave a cool shrug. 'What did you expect?'

'I was hoping you'd have got over it by now. That you'd be glad for me. Maybe even proud of what I accomplished.'

Something moved in his eyes, so that for a moment Kaitlin thought she was getting through to him. But when he spoke his voice was curt. 'Why did you think that?'

'The other women were all so good, if I hadn't worked so hard I wouldn't have been able to compete with them.' And as his expression failed to soften, 'Surely you understand?'

'I ordered you not to ride in the rodeo.'

She had tried to appease him, but this was too much. Kaitlin's head shot up. 'I don't take orders, Flynn, don't you know that by now? Look, I appreciate your concern. I tried to tell you that yesterday.' She paused a moment, before adding in a softer tone, 'Flynn... Flynn, I had to do what I did.'

'Do you really think that, Kaitlin?'

'Yes,' she insisted. 'I'm still optimistic about the cattle sales, but they're more than a month away. The rodeo was my only means of laying my hands on some money quickly.'

Dark eyes raked her face. 'I made you an offer.'

'One I couldn't accept.'

'You made that clear enough,' he said grimly.

This was not going at all the way Kaitlin had hoped. 'Flynn...' she pleaded, 'don't let's argue. I'm still so excited about yesterday, don't spoil it for me. Please?' She put her hand on his arm, and felt hard muscles contract instantly beneath her fingers. 'Come to the house with me. I have your cheque ready, and then—'

He pulled his arm away, as if her touch repelled him. 'Forget it!' he snapped.

Feeling a little ill, Kaitlin stared at him. 'Forget it? Why?'

'I don't want your cheque. Tear it up.'

'I don't understand, Flynn. All these months you've been after me for payment, never once agreeing to give me time when I needed it. Demanding services from me when I didn't have the money to pay. And now you're telling me to tear up my cheque?'

'While you're about it,' Flynn said harshly, 'there's something else you can tear up.'

'What?' His fury had Kaitlin confused.

'This,' he said savagely, thrusting a large brown envelope into her hands.

Kaitlin glanced at it. 'What is this?'

'Open it.'

Kaitlin did as he asked. 'What is this?' she asked again, as she drew several sheets of paper from the envelope.

'What does it look like? Your damned mortgage, of course.'

Kaitlin began to tremble. 'Why… Why did you bring it?'

'It's yours now. Tear it up, Kaitlin.'

This couldn't be happening!

She looked up at Flynn, her eyes dazed. 'There are so many payments still owing.' Her voice shook.

'Tear it up.' He bit out the words.

'How can I? Flynn I don't have the right to—'

'If you won't tear it up, I will.'

Seizing the document from her hand, Flynn ripped it in several pieces.

Bemused, Kaitlin watched the paper shreds drop to the ground. Lifting her head, she looked again at Flynn. The man she loved had never looked tougher, remoter, angrier than he did at this moment.

'I don't understand…'

'It's quite simple. You own your ranch, Kaitlin. Your precious ranch is free of debt.'

A dream, Kaitlin thought feverishly. A pleasant dream by rights—no more mortgage, no more worries!—yet a dream that had the trappings of a nightmare.

'There's something else,' Flynn said.

Kaitlin caught the small box he threw at her. 'What is it?'

'Open it.'

'My God!' she whispered, looking at her grandmother's ring. 'Where did you get this?'

'In the pawnshop where you left it.'

'How did you know?' Her throat was so dry that the words emerged painfully.

'I guessed you were up to something when you made that one payment. I was fairly certain you hadn't sold any cattle, so you must have sold something else, something of value. I scoured every pawnshop in the city until I found this ring.'

'I don't understand… You didn't even know I owned it,' she whispered.

'No, but I had a picture of you, and the man had your name. He showed me the ring.'

'And you bought it back. Flynn... Flynn, thank you. I... I'll find a way of giving you the money.'

'I don't want it!'

'But I must—'

'Forget it!' he ordered.

'And this?' Kaitlin made a wide gesture over the paper-strewn ground. Through dry lips she whispered, 'Why, Flynn? What's this all about?'

Flynn's gaze was savage. 'Simply put, Kaitlin, after what happened yesterday I realized there was no point in continuing to hold the mortgage.'

'Flynn... I don't understand a word of what you're saying.'

'I made you an offer. No more payments, ever. The ranch would be your home. We'd be married. The two weeks away was to have been our honeymoon. You could have had everything you wanted—what I *thought* you wanted. But you shoved the offer back in my face. Treated it as if it was the very worst insult a man could possibly throw at you.'

'Flynn—'

'Let me finish, Kaitlin. It won't take long. After that, you'll be free of me—I'll never burden you with my presence again.'

'Flynn, no...' she said urgently. But as she took a step towards him, he deliberately moved backwards out of her reach.

'I asked you not to ride in the rodeo, Kaitlin. I couldn't bear the thought that you might hurt that lovely face and body. But you wouldn't be stopped. Proud Kaitlin, independent Kaitlin, determined to push yourself to the limits rather than live with a man who repulses you, a man you can't stand.'

'No, Flynn! I don't—'

Once again, he would not let her speak. 'It's not enough that I love you, that I'm crazy about you, that I'd pluck the moon and the stars out of the sky for you if that was what you wanted.'

Happiness exploded inside her. 'What are you saying?' she whispered incredulously.

'I've reached the end of the road. When you insisted on riding in the rodeo, I understood—finally—that there was no point in continuing to pursue a woman who will never love me. Your mortgage won't haunt you any longer, Kaitlin. Nor will I. I will never be back.'

Giving her no time to respond, Flynn turned and leaped into the plane.

Kaitlin stared after him, so stunned by the things he had said that for several seconds she could neither move nor speak. When movement finally returned to her limbs, she ran to the door of the plane.

'*Flynn*!' she shouted. 'Flynn, wait!'

But the door was already closed. If Flynn heard her call, he did not respond. Kaitlin banged on the side of the plane, but in vain. As the engine shot into life, she stepped backwards quickly.

'*Flynn*!' she shouted in anguish as the plane lifted off the ground. '*I love you, Flynn*! *I love you—do you hear me*?'

But the words were lost in a rush of wind. The plane rose in the air, higher and higher, and the pilot did not look back.

Tears spilled from Kaitlin's eyes. Bitterly she wept as the man she adored flew out of her life.

Some time during the night Kaitlin made a decision.

She was up before daybreak. In the cookhouse the cowboys were already at breakfast. Kaitlin called to Brett, the cowboy who had been at the ranch longer than any of the others; loyal Brett, who had stayed around even when times had turned tough and salaries had dipped.

It did not take her long to tell Brett that she was going away for a while—she could not say when she would be back—and that she wanted him to take charge of her ranch in her absence.

Her ranch! It really was hers now. Her beloved home, free of debt, hers to build up to the best of her ability. Her ranch... She should be delirious with happiness—but she wasn't.

On the long drive into the city, Kaitlin relived the things Flynn had said to her yesterday: things that had astonished and elated her. *Flynn loved her—who would have thought it*? But there was also the memory of his terrible anger, and an antagonism so intense that she did not know if anything could defuse it.

Kaitlin drove as fast as the speed limit would allow, only stopping now and then to refuel. On the outskirts of the city, she slowed the car. Flynn had never told her his address—perhaps because she had not thought to ask—and she had no idea where he lived. Fortunately, he was listed in the local telephone directory: a street map showed her how to get there.

The next time Kaitlin stopped the car was outside a row of town houses. The sprawling Spanish-style complex took her by surprise: it was almost impossible to imagine Flynn living anywhere but on a ranch.

Repeated ringing of the doorbell yielded no response, but after a few minutes the door next to Flynn's opened.

'He's out,' Kaitlin was informed by a pleasant elderly woman.

'Do you know when he'll be back?'

'I've no idea, honey. I do know he was flying off someplace. I know because I collect his mail when he's away.'

'No!' Kaitlin exclaimed in consternation. 'Do you know when he left?'

'Not long ago. Maybe half an hour.'

Half an hour... To have driven all this way, only to find Flynn gone. Kaitlin felt ill with disappointment.

The woman was eyeing her curiously. 'Are you all right?'

'...Yes.' Kaitlin swallowed. 'But I do need to speak to Flynn. I'll drive out to the airport, maybe I'll be lucky and find him. Thank you for your help.'

She was turning to go when Flynn's neighbour called her back. 'Miss... He may not be at the airport yet. He said something about needing to buy something first.'

'Do you know where he might have gone?' Kaitlin asked
urgently.

'He said something about jewellery. There are a couple
of jewellery stores in a mall not far from here. Three blocks
east, two blocks south. Do you think you can find your
way?'

'Oh, yes! Thank you, thank you so very much.'

'You can thank me if you find Flynn.' The woman's
smile was warm with encouragement.

The first jewellery store Kaitlin came to had a sale on, and
was crowded, but there was no sign of Flynn. Kaitlin ran
further. Near the end of the mall was another store: the
only customer in it was a man, a broad-shouldered giant of
a man who was looking perplexed as he tried to decide
between three pairs of earrings. Even from a distance,
Kaitlin could see that the earrings matched the necklace she
had worn to the banquet.

Weak with love and relief, she stood quite still a few
seconds, catching her breath as she watched Flynn.

'Can you describe the lady, sir?' a saleswoman was asking him helpfully.

'The loveliest green eyes you ever saw. Golden hair to
her shoulders—when it's not tied back—soft and sweet-
smelling. Very pretty.' Flynn paused before adding, 'Beautiful, actually.'

'I suggest the hanging earrings, sir. If they're not right,
the store has an exchange policy.'

'Maybe...' the rugged cowboy said doubtfully.

Behind him, Kaitlin said, 'I think the lady would adore
the hanging earrings.'

Flynn swung around. '*Kaitlin*!'

'Yes,' she said, over the lump in her throat.

'*What are you doing here*? How did you know where to
find me?'

'Your neighbour told me.'

He was moving towards Kaitlin when the saleswoman
reminded him about the earrings. Her eyes were alive with
curiosity, as if she longed to know what was happening.

'The earrings. Right! Do you really like them, Kaitlin?'

'They're wonderful.'

'Then we'll take them.'

Outside the store, minutes later, Flynn turned to her. 'I can't believe you're here! I was about to leave town.'

'Yes, I know.'

'You seem to know an awful lot,' he said wryly. 'Do you also know where I was going?'

'Your neighbour didn't tell me that.'

Flynn gripped her arms. 'Can't you guess?'

The breath stopped in her throat as she looked up at him. 'Why don't you tell me?'

'I was on my way to the ranch.'

Her heart began a rapid beating. 'With the earrings?'

Flynn's eyes were dark and deep, his lips had never looked more tempting. 'With the earrings,' he confirmed.

'Why, Flynn?'

'I'll tell you—after you've told me why you're here.'

'Flynn…' The words she had rehearsed on her way to the city were forgotten. She could only gaze at the rugged face, while inside her a wild yearning flamed.

'Kaitlin? You must have had a reason for coming all this way.'

Her courage returned. Meeting his eyes, she said softly, 'I did have a reason. I came to tell you… Flynn, I'm in love with you.'

'Kaitlin!' he exclaimed.

'I love you, Flynn.'

'We have to talk.' His voice was ragged. 'We'll go back to my place. I take it you're here by car?' She nodded, and he said, 'And I have to drive my own car back to the town house. Be quick, sweet—but not too quick. You're not used to city traffic and I won't go on living if anything happens to you.'

Tender words from such a tough man. Another lump formed in Kaitlin's throat.

Flynn's neighbour was watering the flowers on her patio when Kaitlin drove up. 'He's back,' she said.

'I know, and I'm so grateful to you for telling me where to find him.'

'I was glad to. He's been looking like a grizzly in a bad mood ever since yesterday, but when I saw him just now that look was gone. He's a good man, a really good man.'

Kaitlin smiled happily at the woman. 'Yes, he is.'

A second after she knocked, the door of the town house was flung open. And then Flynn was pulling her into his arms, holding her close to him, nuzzling his lips in her hair, brushing his tongue over her throat before nibbling each ear in turn.

'What did you say?' he demanded, when he lifted his head at last.

Kaitlin laughed up at him. 'You haven't given me a chance to say anything—yet.'

'Impossible woman! On the street, after we left the store. Tell me I didn't dream the words, Kaitlin.'

Her cheeks were warm. 'That I love you? That was no dream, Flynn.'

He pulled her closer. 'Just when I was almost ready to give up hope, the miracle happens. Do you know, I was about to fly out to the ranch and tell you I'd never take no for an answer? And here you are. Do you really mean it, Kaitlin? Do you really love me, my darling?'

Darling... The word was heavenly music, resonating in her mind and her heart.

'I mean it,' she said softly. 'And you, Flynn... Yesterday you said—'

'That I love you! More than I ever dreamed possible. You're my life, Kaitlin. My blood, my heart, I can't imagine living without you. That's why I wasn't prepared to give up—even after all my angry words yesterday. I was going straight to the airport the moment I left the store.'

'We'd have missed each other.'

'No, we wouldn't, because I'd have stayed at the ranch till you got back. I'd have waited as long as I had to. God, Kaitlin, I can't believe we're here together, that you love me. That we can make a life together.' He held her away from him. 'We can do that, can't we?'

'Flynn...'

'You haven't answered me, darling.'

'I know. But, Flynn—'

'I won't let you turn me down, Kaitlin.'

'I'm not about to. But before we talk about a future, I need to know about the past.'

'The past?' he said slowly.

'The mortgage and your obsession to own the ranch. There's so much I don't understand.'

He held her a moment longer, before putting her from him. They sat down and Flynn said, 'Where do you want me to start?'

'The promise.'

'The promise...' A brooding expression came into Flynn's eyes: he had the look of a man who was going far back in his memories.

'Much of it you already know,' he said at last. 'I made a promise to you, and to myself, that I would return to the ranch five years after leaving it.'

'You were going to own it, one way or another.'

Flynn made a wry face. 'That was my plan at the start. I'm sorry about it now, but that's the way it was.'

'And you were going to have me, as well.'

'Yes. Though that part of the plan only came some time later. After I'd left the ranch, after the short marriage to Elise.'

'Not because you loved me, Flynn.'

'No,' he said quietly, 'I admit that love had nothing to do with it. Not then.'

Over the pain the words brought, she said, 'You were determined to own the ranch at any cost.'

'...That's right.'

'Even if it meant foreclosing on the mortgage.'

'I offered to buy the ranch from you, Kaitlin.'

'And I refused. I couldn't just give in to you.'

'You never gave in on a thing, not a single thing, my brave-spirited Kaitlin.' He leaned over and gave her hand a loving squeeze. 'I thought I'd planned everything so well. What didn't occur to me was that I would fall in love with you all over again. I didn't want to love you, Kaitlin, but perhaps I had never stopped. I think now that's what it was.

I always loved you, and maybe that's why my marriage to Elise had no chance—you were always there in the background, I was never able to push you out of my heart. The thing is, I didn't know it. I'd closed my mind to you. I didn't want to feel anything for you.'

'You were so hostile when you came to the ranch that first day, Flynn. So arrogant. Do you remember how you taunted me?'

'I was wrong,' he said contritely. 'I should never have said the things I did, but I was angry.'

Angry at what, Kaitlin wondered, but did not ask the question. Flynn, she felt sure, would come to the reason for his anger in his own time.

She had been angry, too, of course. But she had had good reason.

Curiously, she said, 'So you didn't want to love me. When did things change?'

'Almost from the start. You weren't the girl I remembered. You were so thin, so care-worn and vulnerable. On that very first day, when we rode out together to rescue the lost calf, you began to break down the wall I'd erected around my heart. Every time I saw you I wanted you more. I found myself wanting to take care of you, needing to protect you. But you were so fiercely independent, so determined to make a go of things on your own.'

'You weren't exactly a pushover, Flynn. My financial position was so desperate, and I kept worrying that you'd take the ranch away from me. You'd have succeeded if you hadn't come up with the idea for services instead of payment.'

The wonderful dark eyes sparkled wickedly. 'The idea wasn't what you thought it was, Kaitlin.'

She stared at him. 'What on earth do you mean?'

'Don't you know, my darling? By the time I suggested the first service, I knew we belonged together. The service idea was my way of letting us spend time together.'

'I was a rich bitch who knew how to shop.'

'No, darling, it was never that. Going shopping together was one way of wooing you.'

'Good heavens!' Kaitlin said in amazement. 'And I never

guessed.' She looked at him. 'But, Flynn, you *did* say I was spoiled rotten, that I knew my way around clothing stores.'

'You insisted on knowing why I'd take you shopping in exchange for payment, and that seemed as good an excuse as any. We did have fun, didn't we, darling?'

'Oh yes, Flynn, we did. That first day in the city, when we bought you all those clothes for the oilmen's convention, that was great.'

'And the second trip, when we bought the green grown.'

'Which was meant for another woman.'

'There was never anyone else, darling. The gown was always for you, as was the necklace.'

'But you said…' Kaitlin thought back. 'Flynn, you said you were taking a woman to the banquet.'

Flynn laughed softly. 'I didn't tell you the woman's name. You assumed there was someone else, and I let you believe it. I even hoped you'd be jealous.'

'I was,' Kaitlin admitted ruefully. The admission was easy now. 'I hated that woman.'

He laughed. 'So I gathered.'

'And all the while I loved wearing the gown and the necklace. There were times when I even forgot they weren't really mine.'

'Everything seemed to go so well at the banquet. Our night together afterwards was especially fantastic. I thought I was in heaven when we made love.'

Kaitlin hesitated a moment, then said softly, 'I felt that way, too.'

'Until things turned sour. I've never understood what went wrong, Kaitlin. Why were you so angry?'

'I thought you'd used me, Flynn. When you talked about letting me off additional payments, I felt cheap and abused. I…I thought you were buying me.'

'*Buying you*!' Flynn laughed remorsefully. 'Kaitlin, my darling, it was never that. I was going to ask you again to marry me. For all the right reasons this time. I had made up my mind not to take no for an answer—but you threw me out of your room first.'

Kaitlin was stunned. 'I had no idea!'

'I considered proposing to you anyway, but you were so

furious, I knew you'd reject me outright. Which meant I had to change my plans.'

'Flynn?' Kaitlin said uncertainly.

'What did you think, my darling, when I asked you to pack a suitcase? When I told you we'd be away for two weeks? That I was planning to use you again?'

'Yes,' she admitted.

'But I asked you to marry me.'

'You don't know how tempting the offer was, my darling—' there she had said the words, too, and what bliss it was to feel them roll from her tongue '—but to say yes to marriage when I believed that you despised me... I couldn't do it, Flynn.'

'So that's why you said no.'

'Of course.'

'At least now you know the truth.'

'Not about everything.' Kaitlin ached with the longing to throw herself into Flynn's arms. But she said, 'There are still things we haven't talked about.'

'Such as?'

'I don't know why you left the ranch five years ago.'

His expression changed, becoming remote and a little forbidding. 'You've taken your time asking me that.'

'Not because I haven't wanted to—I have, many times— but until today I've never felt comfortable enough.' Despite Flynn's altered mood, she pressed on. 'I had that party. And the next morning you left. Flynn—why?'

'Perhaps,' he said evenly, 'you should tell me what you think happened that night.'

'You know all about it.'

'I thought I did. Now I want to hear it in your words.'

The mood in the room had changed. There was tension in the air now. Kaitlin felt nervous and on edge. She was reluctant to talk about the fateful evening so long ago— and knew she had no choice. She told him everything.

'Finally,' she said, 'I got one of the cowboys to go to town with me and help me find you. I'd been dreaming of the party, Flynn, and I was going to spend it with the man I loved. I even thought that we might announce our engagement. Instead...' She stopped.

When she went on, her voice was bitter. 'Can you imagine how I felt when I found you in that bar? Sitting in an alcove, with that red-haired woman in your arms. I... I wanted to die, Flynn. I asked you what you were doing, and you said, ''What does it look like?'' and then you kissed her.'

She was silent a few moments before she spoke again. 'That's it, Flynn, the whole story. You let me down on the night that was so important to me. And with that awful woman. I've never known why you did it.'

'What did you think, Kaitlin?' His voice was so odd.

'There was only one reason I could come up with. I wouldn't let you make love to me until after the party. Did you reject me because you thought I was playing too hard to get?'

'It was nothing like that, Kaitlin.'

'Are you sure you're not just saying that now?'

'Quite sure.'

Flynn pushed his hand through his hair in a gesture that was becoming achingly familiar. 'I think,' he said, 'that it's time you heard my version of what happened that night.'

'Does it differ from mine?'

'I'll let you answer that when I've finished. Do you know that I went off on a cattle drive?'

'The day after you washed my back. Of course, I remember, Flynn. You didn't say a word about going. That was when I first began to wonder whether you were rejecting me.'

'I couldn't tell you,' he said, looking grim. 'The order came without any warning. The other cowboys had known for a week that they were going, I knew nothing until ten minutes before we started out, and by then it was too late to get in touch with you.'

'You were given such short notice? Wasn't that a bit odd?'

'Not when I'd had time to think about it. Your parents knew I was in the house with you that day, Kaitlin.'

'They didn't say anything to me.'

'Are you certain?'

'...Yes.'

'Think back, darling. Your parents must have said *something* when they came back from town that afternoon and found you in the bath.'

'It's so long ago, Flynn. Still, I remember… I remember my mother made some comment about all the water on the floor.' She looked up. 'Come to think of it, she did seem a bit suspicious. She asked me if I had anything to tell her.'

'Did you admit that I was with you?'

'No, and she didn't press me. If she had, I think I would have had to tell her the truth.'

'All the same, your mother knew, Kaitlin. Both your parents did. I dashed out through the back door just as they were coming in the front. I was almost certain your dad spotted me.'

'I'm sure you're wrong about that, Flynn—if they'd known, they'd have said something.'

'They took action instead. I was sent on the cattle drive, and that kept us apart for a week.'

'I never guessed… never dreamed…' Kaitlin paused. On a harder note, she went on. 'You were back at the ranch in time for the party. I know because I was at the bunk-house: you were showering, and with the first guests arriving, there was no time for me to go back. Anyway, I didn't think it was necessary—you knew I was expecting you. It never occurred to me that you'd decide not to come.'

'I was at your party, Kaitlin.' Flynn gave her a level look.

She looked back at him, stunned. 'I didn't see you!'

'I was there. Hair slicked back, wearing new clothes bought specially for the occasion. I also had something else that was new, Kaitlin.'

For some reason his tone made her tense. 'What was it, Flynn?'

'A ring. A tiny ring, darling, but it cost me all the money I had saved.' The dark eyes held hers, defying them to break the mutual gaze. 'I was going to ask you to marry me.'

'What I was hoping for! What happened, Flynn?'

'I was turned away at the door.'

'*No!*' An anguished cry.

'You don't believe me?'

'Who would have done such a thing, Flynn?'

But even as she spoke, Kaitlin was able to guess the answer.

'Your parents were both at the door. Your father told me, very politely, that I wasn't welcome. Without quite saying so, he made me understand that the party wasn't for cowboys.'

'*You* knew better than that, Flynn. You knew I'd invited you. You didn't have to accept what Dad said.'

'I tried to argue, to explain, but without success. Your mother implied that you'd only invited me to the party because you didn't want to appear snobbish or rude. She said it was nice that I was teaching you to ride, but that I shouldn't mistake your affectionate manner for anything deeper.'

'You should have known it wasn't true! You could have insisted on coming into the house.'

'I tried, Kaitlin. Your mother told me to look through the doorway. And there you were, dancing with a handsome fair-haired guy. You were laughing with him. And then the two of you kissed.'

'No,' Kaitlin protested. 'Perhaps that was how it looked to you, but it must have been *he* who did the kissing, not the other way around. It's all so long ago, Flynn, I haven't the faintest idea who the guy was or why he kissed me. I do know it couldn't have been anything serious.'

Dark eyes gleamed. 'Am I supposed to believe that?'

'Yes! But, Flynn, whatever my parents may have said, you knew I was expecting you.'

'I knew you'd been to the bunk-house, the other cowboys told me that. When I saw you with the fair-haired man, I got to thinking that maybe you'd had second thoughts about inviting me to the party, that your reason for going to the bunk-house was because you wanted to tell me not to come.'

'What a misunderstanding!'

'I left the party, but I came back. I looked in through the windows. You were having a good time, Kaitlin, surrounded by a crowd of people who were all so different from me. For the first time I realized what I should have understood all along—you and I were from different worlds. Things could never work out between us.'

'I don't agree!'

'At that moment I thought your parents might be right.'

'And you thought I was a snob?' Kaitlin asked incredulously. 'If I hadn't wanted you at my party, I would never have invited you in the first place. I was crazy about you, Flynn—you knew that.'

'When a man is bitter, my darling, he tells himself all sorts of things. I decided you'd been enjoying yourself with me only because there was nobody else around. I thought you were a flirt without a conscience; that I'd allowed myself to believe we could have a future, when nothing was further from your mind.'

'And so you went to town, and had sex with that awful woman.'

'I needed to drown my sorrows. A few drinks in the bar seemed like a good way of putting you out of my mind. The woman, Marietta, was happy to keep me company.' Flynn shot her a wicked grin. 'I didn't have sex with her, darling. Even then, when I was so mad with you, I knew I couldn't touch another woman.'

'You were cuddling,' Kaitlin accused.

'No, darling, we were not. I saw you come in, and I pulled her onto my lap. She was a good sort, she knew I was feeling hellish, and she was happy to go along with the act.'

'Flynn, there's one thing that doesn't make sense.'

'What's that, sweet?'

'If I hadn't wanted you at my party, why would I have gone to the trouble of finding you in town?'

'That didn't occur to me until some time afterwards. When I did think about it, I put it down to hurt pride on your part.'

'It wasn't my pride that was hurt, it was my heart. And then, the morning after the party you left the ranch.'

'I couldn't stay, Kaitlin—not when I knew I'd have to see you every day, and that we could never have a life together. I was very angry, so the decision wasn't difficult.'

Curiously, Kaitlin said, 'And the promise—did you really believe that you would own the ranch some day?'

'Filled with ambition and a desire for revenge, yes I meant it. Can you forgive me for that, darling?'

'Now that I know what happened—yes. Flynn... Darling...' She paused, then said awkwardly, 'About my parents. I'm really sorry they treated you so badly. I guess they were just trying to do what they thought was best for me. What they did was terrible, but they loved me, Flynn.'

'And I love you, too, my darling. More than I can ever tell you in words.' He reached out his arms to her. 'Come to me, Kaitlin.'

She went to him willingly. He held her on his lap, the big cowboy, hard-muscled and tough, yet incredibly tender, cuddling her against him. It was bliss to sit with him like that.

After a while he said, 'You still haven't answered my question.'

Her heartbeats escalated. 'Why don't you repeat it, Flynn?'

'My darling Kaitlin, will you marry me?'

'Yes, Flynn, of course I will.' Tears welled in her eyes but she lifted her head a little away from him, so that she could look into his face. 'I love you, darling, so much, and I want to be your wife.'

'Kaitlin. My precious love.' His voice was ragged.

'You've always been my love, Flynn, there's never been anyone else.'

'I have tickets booked for a trip, Kaitlin. Our honeymoon. A Caribbean cruise. A cowboy on a boat—can you imagine?'

'Sounds heavenly,' Kaitlin said as she reached up and kissed him.

'Will the ranch be OK, darling?'

'Oh, yes, I asked Brett to look after it for me. I told him I didn't know how long I'd be gone.'

A while later—kissing took time—Flynn said, 'We'll live on the ranch, Kaitlin?'

'Yes, darling.'

'Your ranch, my love. I meant it when I tore up the mortgage.'

'Ours,' she corrected him.

'Not after what I put you through. I don't want you to wonder, ever, whether I married you to get my hands on the ranch.'

'I'll never think that,' she promised him. 'It will be our home, darling. It already is.'

'Sweet Kaitlin, do you know that I plan to spend the rest of my life showing you how much I love you?'

'Starting when?' she asked mischievously.

'Now,' Flynn said, as he lifted her into his arms and carried her to his bedroom.

MILLS & BOON®

Next Month's Romances

Each month you can choose from a wide variety of romance novels from Mills & Boon. Below are the new titles to look out for next month from the Presents™ and Enchanted™ series.

Presents™

THE DIAMOND BRIDE	Carole Mortimer
THE SHEIKH'S SEDUCTION	Emma Darcy
THE SEDUCTION PROJECT	Miranda Lee
THE UNMARRIED HUSBAND	Cathy Williams
THE TEMPTATION GAME	Kate Walker
THE GROOM'S DAUGHTER	Natalie Fox
HIS PERFECT WIFE	Susanne McCarthy
A FORBIDDEN MARRIAGE	Margaret Mayo

Enchanted™

BABY IN A MILLION	Rebecca Winters
MAKE BELIEVE ENGAGEMENT	Day Leclaire
THE WEDDING PROMISE	Grace Green
A MARRIAGE WORTH KEEPING	Kate Denton
TRIAL ENGAGEMENT	Barbara McMahon
ALMOST A FATHER	Pamela Bauer & Judy Kaye
MARRIED BY MISTAKE!	Renee Roszel
THE TENDERFOOT	Patricia Knoll

H1 9802

Available from WH Smith, John Menzies, Martins, Tesco and Asda

PARTY TIME!

How would you like to win a year's supply of Mills & Boon® Books? Well, you can and they're FREE! Simply complete the competition below and send it to us by 31st August 1998. The first five correct entries picked after the closing date will each win a year's subscription to the Mills & Boon series of their choice. What could be easier?

BALLOONS	BUFFET	ENTERTAIN
STREAMER	DANCING	INVITE
DRINKS	CELEBRATE	FANCY DRESS
MUSIC	PARTIES	HANGOVER

S	O	E	T	A	R	B	E	L	E	C
T	E	F	M	U	S	I	C	D	D	H
S	U	I	V	Z	T	E	Y	R	A	A
N	E	N	T	E	R	T	A	I	N	N
O	B	V	E	R	E	H	K	N	C	G
O	J	I	F	O	A	L	R	K	I	O
L	M	T	F	V	M	P	U	S	N	V
L	P	E	U	Q	E	N	Z	S	G	E
A	W	G	B	X	R	C	T	B	Y	R
B	F	A	N	C	Y	D	R	E	S	S

C8B

Please turn over for details of how to enter...

HOW TO ENTER

Can you find our twelve party words? They're all hidden somewhere in the grid. They can be read backwards, forwards, up, down or diagonally. As you find each word in the grid put a line through it. When you have completed your wordsearch, don't forget to fill in the coupon below, pop this page into an envelope and post it today—you don't even need a stamp!

Mills & Boon Party Time! Competition
FREEPOST CN81, Croydon, Surrey, CR9 3WZ
EIRE readers send competition to PO Box 4546, Dublin 24.

Please tick the series you would like to receive if you are one of the lucky winners

Presents™ ❑ Enchanted™ ❑ Medical Romance™ ❑
Historical Romance™ ❑ Temptation® ❑

Are you a Reader Service™ Subscriber?   Yes ❑   No ❑

Mrs/Ms/Miss/Mr ....Intials ....(BLOCK CAPITALS PLEASE)

Surname...

Address ....

....

..................................Postcode..........................

(I am over 18 years of age)   C8B

One application per household. Competition open to residents of the UK and Ireland only. You may be mailed with offers from other reputable companies as a result of this application. If you would prefer not to receive such offers, please tick box. ❑

Closing date for entries is 31st August 1998.

Mills & Boon® is a registered trademark of Harlequin Mills & Boon Limited.

MILLS & BOON®

Relive the romance with

Bestselling themed romances brought back to you by popular demand

Each month By Request brings you three full-length novels in one beautiful volume featuring the best of the best.

So if you missed a favourite Romance the first time around, here is your chance to relive the magic from some of our most popular authors.

Look out for
Nine to Five **in February 1998 by Jessica Steele, Susan Napier and Lindsay Armstrong**

Available from WH Smith, John Menzies, Martins and Tesco

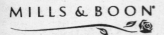

MILLS & BOON®

SPECIAL OFFER £5 OFF

FLYING FLOWERS

Beautiful fresh flowers, sent by 1st class post to any UK and Eire address.

™ **SILHOUETTE**®

We have teamed up with Flying Flowers, the UK's premier 'flowers by post' company, to offer you £5 off a choice of their two most popular bouquets the 18 mix (CAS) of 10 multihead and 8 luxury bloom Carnations and the 25 mix (CFG) of 15 luxury bloom Carnations, 10 Freesias and Gypsophila. All bouquets contain fresh flowers 'in bud', added greenery, bouquet wrap, flower food, care instructions, and personal message card. They are boxed, gift wrapped and sent by 1st class post.

To redeem £5 off a Flying Flowers bouquet, simply complete the application form below and send it with your cheque or postal order to; **HMB Flying Flowers Offer, The Jersey Flower Centre, Jersey JE1 5FF.**

ORDER FORM (Block capitals please) Valid for delivery anytime until 30th November 1998 MAB/0198/A

Title .... Initials .... Surname ....

Address ....

....

....Postcode ....

Signature ....Are you a Reader Service Subscriber **YES/NO**

Bouquet(s) **18 CAS** (Usual Price £14.99) **£9.99** ☐   **25 CFG** (Usual Price £19.99) **£14.99** ☐

I enclose a cheque/postal order payable to Flying Flowers for £ .... or payment by

VISA/MASTERCARD ☐☐☐☐ ☐☐☐☐ ☐☐☐☐ ☐☐☐☐ Expiry Date ..../........../

PLEASE SEND MY BOUQUET TO ARRIVE BY ..../........../

TO Title .... Initials .... Surname ....

Address ....

....

....Postcode ....

Message (Max 10 Words) ....

Please allow a minimum of four working days between receipt of order and 'required by date' for delivery.

You may be mailed with offers from other reputable companies as a result of this application.
Please tick box if you would prefer not to receive such offers. ☐

Terms and Conditions Although dispatched by 1st class post to arrive by the required date the exact day of delivery cannot be guaranteed. Valid for delivery anytime until 30th November 1998. Maximum of 5 redemptions per household, photocopies of the voucher will be accepted.